Praise for Yan Lianke

"Yan is one of those rare geniuses who finds in the peculiar absurdities of his own culture the absurdities that infect all cultures."
—*Washington Post*

"Yan's subject is China, but he has condensed the human forces driving today's global upheavals into a bracing, universal vision."
—*New York Times*

"China's most controversial novelist ... [A] preternatural gift for metaphor spills out of him unbidden."—*New Yorker*

"One of China's eminent and most controversial novelists and satirists."
—*Chicago Tribune*

"China's foremost literary satirist.... [Yan] deploys offbeat humour, anarchic set pieces and surreal imagery to shed new light on dark episodes from modern Chinese history."—*Financial Times*

"One of China's most important—and certainly most fearless—living writers."—*Kirkus Reviews*

"A master of imaginative satire."—*Guardian*

DISCOVERING FICTION

SINOTHEORY

A series edited by Carlos Rojas and Eileen Cheng-yin Chow

Yan Lianke
DISCOVERING FICTION

TRANSLATED AND WITH AN INTRODUCTION BY
CARLOS ROJAS

DUKE UNIVERSITY PRESS
Durham and London 2022

© 2011 发现小说 Yan Lianke
© 2022 Introduction and English Translation,
Duke University Press
All rights reserved
Printed in the United States of America on
acid-free paper ∞
Designed by A. Mattson Gallagher
Typeset in Adobe Jenson Pro and Futura Std
by Westchester Publishing Services

Library of Congress Cataloging-in-Publication Data
Names: Yan Lianke, [date] author. | Rojas, Carlos, [date]
translator.
Title: Discovering fiction / Yan Lianke ; translated by
Carlos Rojas.
Other titles: Fa xian xiao shuo. English | Sinotheory.
Description: Durham : Duke University Press, 2022. |
Series: Sinotheory | Includes bibliographical references
and index.
Identifiers: LCCN 2021041141 (print) | LCCN 2021041142
(ebook)
ISBN 9781478015673 (hardcover)
ISBN 9781478018308 (paperback)
ISBN 9781478022916 (ebook)
Subjects: LCSH: Fiction—Technique. | Fiction—History
and criticism. | Realism in literature. | BISAC: LITERARY CRITI-
CISM / General | FICTION / Literary
Classification: LCC PL2925.L54 F3613 2022 (print) |
LCC PL2925.L54 (ebook) | DDC 895.13/52—dc23/
eng/20220111
LC record available at https://lccn.loc.gov/2021041141
LC ebook record available at https://lccn.loc.gov/2021041142

Cover art: Zhong Biao, *Take Off*, 2015. Oil on
canvas, 59 × 47¼ inches (150 × 120 cm). Courtesy
of Eli Klein Gallery and the artist; © Zhong Biao.

Contents

Translator's Introduction
Creating Reality and Surpassing Realism

CARLOS ROJAS

Completed in 2010 (and published in 2011), *Discovering Fiction* opens with a reference to "A Traitor to Writing," Yan Lianke's afterword to his 2010 novel *The Four Books*. Set in a re-education camp for accused Rightists in the late 1950s, the novel explores not only the political persecution associated with the Anti-Rightist Campaign (1957–1959) but also the devastating famine that took the lives of tens of millions of Chinese during this same period. Known euphemistically as the "three years of natural disaster," the Great Famine (1959–1962) was actually a direct result of a set of misguided political and economic policies implemented under the Great Leap Forward Campaign (1958–1962).

Although the Anti-Rightist Campaign and the Great Famine impacted wide swaths of China's population, they have received relatively little direct attention by Chinese fiction authors. During the Maoist period, up through the end of the Cultural Revolution (1966–1976), the government exercised strict control over literary production, and even after these controls were loosened during the Reform and Opening Up Campaign that Mao's successor Deng Xiaoping launched in 1978, certain politically sensitive topics remained effectively off-limits—due to a combination of official censorship (whereby all published fiction must be reviewed and approved by government-appointed agents) and soft censorship (whereby authors and publishers are encouraged to voluntarily avoid sensitive topics).

When Yan Lianke mentions at the beginning of *Discovering Fiction* that *The Four Books* "has almost no chance of being published in China," accordingly, this is a reference to his decision to devote the novel to the overlapping political and humanitarian crises that afflicted China in the late 1950s. Yan Lianke had previously had several works that were either banned or recalled (such as *Serve the People!*), or that had been significantly shaped by his own practice of self-censorship (such as *Dream of Ding Village*, which was later recalled anyway). With *The Four Books*, however, Yan Lianke decided to write the novel without consideration of whether it would be acceptable to Chinese publishers and censors. Like many of this works, it was published in Chinese in Taiwan and Hong Kong and was subsequently translated into many foreign languages, but it was never officially published in Mainland China.

Like all of Yan Lianke's fiction, *The Four Books* is closely engaged with the historical realities of modern China, though it frequently approaches these topics in an unusual, fantastic manner. For instance, during the height of the famine, the work's protagonist, who is known simply as "the Author," begins cultivating a secret plot of grain and comes up with the idea of irrigating the soil with his own blood:

> When I lowered my head, I saw that the wheat leaves were covered with a combination of beads of blood and drops of water, and the fields were flowing with a mixture of blood and rain that alternated between light and dark red, as though it were a dyeing mill. I saw the uppermost grain of wheat sucking the blood rain like an infant sucking milk, and the wheat leaves sprinkling drops of blood-water in all directions. After the thick smell of blood dissipated and mixed with the scent of wheat, I became surrounded by a fresh new aroma.
>
> I resolved to slice my own flesh.
>
> I also decided to allow my blood to fully bleed out, to the point that I could no longer remain upright. I collapsed limply to the ground and closed my eyes for a while. When I opened them again, light from the setting sun was shining in through the lower part of the window, like red rain flowing into the room. (293)

The result is a crop of oversized, blood-filled ears of wheat, which are pursued intently by other residents of the re-education camp. Although clearly fantastic, this "blood grain" plotline evocatively captures the sorts of desperate measures to which many victims of the Great Famine were driven.

Similarly, the authorities' attempts to root out and eliminate "Rightist" political and cultural tendencies is manifested, in the novel, in a practice wherein the leader of the re-education camp—a mysterious figure who is identified only as "the Child"—confiscates virtually all of the detainees' books, including both Chinese and Western works, and ritualistically burns them in a giant bonfire. Early in the novel, there is a description of how

> the Child grabbed several volumes, including *Call to Arms, Faust,* and *The Hunchback of Notre Dame,* and lit them on fire. He took a copy of *The Phenomenology of Spirit,* and set it on fire. He took copies of *The Divine Comedy* and *Strange Tales from the Liao Zhai Studio,* and set them on fire as well. The Child burned many books. As he was about to burn Balzac's novels, however, he threw them back onto the pile. And when he was about to burn Tolstoy's novels, he also tossed them onto the pile. He tossed back a copy of *Crime and Punishment,* and said to those two youngsters, "Keep these, and take them all to my house. I can burn them in the winter to keep warm." (17)

It is not until near the end of the novel, meanwhile, that it is finally revealed that the reason why, in this passage, the Child sets aside Honoré de Balzac's and Leo Tolstoy's works is not, as he claims, because he plans to burn them himself, but rather because he is in the process of amassing an enormous private library that includes a copy of virtually every title that he has been publicly confiscating and destroying.

Notably, Balzac and Tolstoy are also crucial reference points in Yan Lianke's detailed discussion, in *Discovering Fiction,* of nineteenth-century European realism, and his study also references many of the other targeted authors and works mentioned in this passage from *The Four Books*—including not only Western classics like *The Hunchback of Notre Dame* but also late imperial Chinese classics such as Pu Songling's *Strange Tales from the Liao Zhai Studio* and early twentieth-century classics such as Lu Xun's short story collection *Call to Arms.* Indeed, the Child's compulsive practice of collecting and storing an eclectic array of literary texts (both premodern and modern, Chinese and Western) may be seen as a compelling metaphor for Yan Lianke's own reading practice;

and in *Discovering Fiction*, Yan offers a thoughtful reflection on how he views his relationship to earlier literary traditions—particularly to nineteenth-century European high realism, early twentieth-century modernism, mid-twentieth-century Latin American magic realism, and the more ideologically inflected tradition of socialist realism (or, what Yan Lianke calls here "constructed realism") that was dominant during the Maoist period.

Born in 1958 in rural Henan, Yan Lianke joined the People's Liberation Army (PLA) in 1978, the same year Deng Xiaoping launched the Reform and Opening Up Campaign, and he published his first story in 1979. Working as a professional author for the PLA, Yan initially focused on writing social realist–style works designed to improve soldier morale. The result was a set of works that resembled socialist realism, in contrast to the avant-garde experimentations of some of contemporaries, such as Yu Hua, Su Tong, Wang Anyi, and Can Xue. Yan Lianke began to gain broader recognition in the late 1980s and early 1990s with a series of six novellas set in the fictional village of Yaogou, and which were republished in 1991 as a single volume under the title *The Prison of Emotion*. The novellas, known collectively as his Yaogou series, are each narrated in the voice of a young man named Yan Lianke, like the author himself—anticipating the metafictional turn that Yan's fiction would take in the late 1990s and 2000s.

In the late 1990s, Yan Lianke began to develop an increasingly experimental writing style that used dark humor to explore a set of underlying social realities. For instance, *Streams of Time* (1998) features a village whose residents suffer from a variety of afflictions—including darkened teeth, joint disease, skeletal deformities, and paralysis—and who all end up dying from throat tumors before they turn forty. The novel was inspired by China's so-called cancer villages, though this term did not enter common usage in China until after the novel was published.[1] *Hard Like Water* (2001) is set during the Cultural Revolution and focuses on a nexus of political passion and libidinal desire, while *Lenin's Kisses* (2004) revolves around a village where virtually all the residents are handicapped, offering a suggestive commentary on the marginalized status of the disabled in contemporary China. Finally, *Dream of*

Ding Village (2006) is set in a village ravaged by AIDS, taking inspiration from the HIV/AIDS epidemic that had devastated rural regions of central China—and particularly Yan Lianke's home province of Henan.

Although each of the preceding works takes inspiration from reality, they all employ an innovative narrative structure and incorporate explicitly fantastic elements. The chapters of *Streams of Time*, for instance, are organized in reverse chronological order; *Lenin's Kisses* features countless endnotes that explain dialectal words and phrases but also offer an important back story to the work's plot; and *Dream of Ding Village* is narrated by a dead boy from beyond the grave. Through these unconventional narrative frames, these works underscore the significance not only of the social realities being represented but also of the process of literary representation itself.

After *Dream of Ding Village*, Yan Lianke published several novels that each foreground authors or scholars. First, *Ballad, Hymn, Ode* (2008) is a satire of Chinese academia that uses a focus on a peasant-turned-scholar to expose a pattern of academic corruption. Two years later, Yan published *The Four Books* (2010), which revolves around a novelist identified as "the Author" who is recruited to compile reports on the other members of the camp and submit them to the authorities. *The Explosion Chronicles* (2013), meanwhile, features a Beijing-based novelist named Yan Lianke, who has been commissioned to compile and edit a local history of his hometown of Explosion, which during the post-Mao period had quickly developed from a modest village into a town, a county, a city, and finally into a provincial-level megalopolis. Similarly, *The Day the Sun Died* (2015) features an eccentric author named Yan Lianke who repeatedly quotes from his own works and is positioned as a suggestive counterpoint to the young boy—and aspiring author— who is the novel's narrator and nominal protagonist. In this way, each of these works focuses on the mediated relationship between reality and literary representation, and specifically on the factors that may influence the direction of the resulting texts. In addition, a more specific theme that runs through several of these recent works involves the sociopolitical forces that may help shape the content of a literary work or restrict its availability to the reading public—and it is no coincidence that during this same period, Yan Lianke's own works became subject to tighter oversight within China.

In *Discovering Fiction*, Yan Lianke offers a systematic overview of literary representation in China and the West, culminating in a discussion of what he calls "mythorealism." Identifying mythorealism as the style of realism that he has followed in his most recent novels, Yan Lianke traces the style's approaches in earlier works by figures ranging from Franz Kafka to Gabriel García Márquez, and defines it as the process of rejecting

> the superficial logical relations that exist in real life in order to explore a kind of invisible and "nonexistent" truth—a truth that is obscured by truth itself. Mythorealism is distinct from conventional realism, and its relationship to reality is not driven by direct causality but instead involves a person's soul and spirit (which is to say, the connection between a person and the real relationship between spirit and interior objects), and an author's conjectures grounded in a real foundation. Mythorealism is not a bridge offering direct access to truth and reality, and instead it relies on imaginings, allegories, myths, legends, dreamscapes, and magical transformations that grow out of the soil of daily life and social reality.

With respect to mythorealism's relationship to realism and reality, Yan Lianke explains that "mythorealism does not definitely reject reality, but attempts to *create reality and surpass realism*" (emphasis added). The phrase Yan Lianke deploys here for "surpass realism" (*chaoyue xianshizhuyi*) closely resembles the Chinese term for "surrealism" (*chaoxianshizhuyi*) but uses the verb *chaoyue* ("to surpass") instead of the prefix *chao* ("sur-"). In a couple of commentaries on *Lenin's Kisses*, meanwhile, we find two alternate ways of understanding the expression *surpassing realism* and, by extension, Yan Lianke's concept of mythorealism itself.

First, in an interview conducted shortly after the publication of *Lenin's Kisses*, the literary critic Li Tuo opens with a lengthy question in which he posits that *Lenin's Kisses* contains "many elements and techniques that appear sur-real [*chaoxianshi*] (though not exactly in the sense of surrealism [*chaoxianshizhuyi*]), and as the plot progresses, these elements and techniques become intimately intertwined with a realistic drive, as a result of which the narrative becomes filled with tensions and contradictions." Li Tuo then offers a detailed overview of various realistic and "sur-realistic" trends in twentieth-century Chinese literature, to which Yan Lianke responds by expressing general agreement with this summary, concluding, "I think we have no choice but to use non-realistic writing practices, just as we have no choice but to use a set of sur-realistic writing practices. It is only by using these sorts of non-realistic and sur-realistic writing practices that it is thereby possible to approximate the kernel of reality and to display the inner core of life."[2]

Here, Yan Lianke follows Li Tuo's lead in describing his literary approach as being "sur-realistic," in the sense of attempting to represent the "sur-real," or a level of reality positioned outside of what is traditionally viewed as the real. Although this sur-realistic approach is not realistic in the sense of representing reality as it is conventionally conceived, it nevertheless attempts to capture a deeper truth by changing the way that we perceive reality itself.

Second, in his 2004 afterword to *Lenin's Kisses*, titled "Seeking a Reality beyond 'Isms,'" Yan Lianke had previously offered an alternate characterization of his novel's relationship to realism when he asked his readers,

> Really, please pay no heed to grandiose discussions of "reality," truth," "art deriving from life," "life is the only source of literary creation," and so forth. In reality, there is no true life laid out in front of you. Every reality, every instance of reality, after having been filtered through an author's mind, inevitably becomes false. When true blood flows through an author's pen, it is inevitably transformed into ink. Truth does not exist in life, and even less does it appear within fiery reality. Instead, truth only exists in the hearts of a select group of authors. That which derives from the heart and the soul is truth, strength, and realism. Even if what grows out of one's inner heart is merely a tiny weed that does not exist in the mortal world, this will nevertheless still be a true mushroom of immortality. This is the reality of writing—a reality that transcends ideology. If one insists on raising the banner of realism, then this would have to be regarded as the only true realism—a realism that surpasses "isms" [*chaoyue zhuyi de xianshizhuyi*].[3]

In this earlier afterword, we find a subtle shift in terminology—from the title's initial reference to an attempt to find "a *reality* beyond 'isms,'" to the essay's more provocative allusion to an attempt to find "a *realism* beyond 'isms'" (emphases added). In this allusion to an effort to move beyond "isms" we find an echo of Gao Xingjian's concept of *meiyou-zhuyi*, which could be translated as either "without isms" (referring to the attempt to distance oneself from existing ideological formations) or as "nothing-ism" (wherein the attempt to disavow ideological formations becomes a new ideological formation in its own right).[4] Indeed, just as Terry Eagleton contends that the Romantic ideal of an aesthetic sphere located outside of ideology is itself a thoroughly ideological conceit,[5] Gao Xingjian's appeal to a nonideological realm "without isms" is itself an ideological gesture.[6] In Yan Lianke's case, meanwhile, what we find is not so much an attempt to access a reality outside of ideology but rather a representational process ("realism") that attempts to break from a set of normalized ideological formations ("isms"). The result is a literary practice that does not imagine itself as being outside of ideology but rather attempts to reassess the relationship between reality, ideology, and literary production.

If we read Yan Lianke's formulation of mythorealism in *Discovering Fiction* through the lens of these two earlier discussions, accordingly, we find two potential understandings of his description of mythorealism's attempt to create reality through a practice that focuses on an attempt "to create reality [and] surpass realism" (*chuangzao xianshi, chaoyue xianshizhuyi*). On one hand, we could follow the lead of Yan Lianke's interview with Li Tuo and understand the phrase in question as describing mythorealism's efforts to create reality and pursue a representational practice that goes beyond conventional reality. On the other hand, if we instead follow the lead of Yan's afterword to *Lenin's Kisses*, we could parse the same phrase as pointing to mythorealism's attempt to create reality and pursue a representational practice that goes beyond *conventional realism* itself.

1 Realism's Four Levels of Truth

1 I AM REALISM'S UNFILIAL SON

I am realism's unfilial son. This is a line I wrote in an afterword titled "A Traitor to Writing" for my novel *The Four Books*—a work that now has almost no chance of ever being published in China. In this afterword, I described how

> I hesitated for a long time before finally calling myself "a traitor to writing." I hesitated because this label is simply too great of an honor, of which I know that I'm certainly unworthy—the same way that Lu Xun's Ah Q was unworthy of being recognized as a member of the Zhao clan. However, the reason I ultimately decided to include this line here is because it occurred to me that many of the deviations from "literary conventions" that appear in *The Four Books* are not true cases of betrayal, but rather are merely preliminary clues—hints of what I might write in the future. This, accordingly, is why I ultimately decided to call myself a traitor to writing.[1]

I've always entertained a fantasy of being able to write whatever I want, without having to consider whether the resulting work would ever be published. *The Four Books* was a partial attempt to write in this sort of unfettered manner, without any thought of publication. When I speak of the possibility of writing in an unfettered manner, I am not referring simply to the possibility of taking a garden plot full of old stories and sowing it with an assortment of coarse and fine grains, full moons and beautiful flowers, chicken droppings and dog shit—which readers might well scorn. Instead, what I mean is that I would like to be able to tell a story exactly as I wish, even at the risk of sounding pretentious or utterly nonsensical. I want for my vocabulary and plotlines to become truly liberated, thereby permitting the creation of a new narrative structure—which is every author's dream. I treated the composition of *The Four Books* as a beautiful vacation from my usual life of writing. During this vacation everything would belong to me—I would be an emperor, and no longer a slave to my pen.

And this is precisely what I did. I endeavored to become a virtual emperor, and a traitor to writing.

From these idle ramblings, one may observe the urgency with which I attempted to escape from certain literary conventions to the point of becoming indignant, biased, and even arrogant. Why is this? When I was preparing to write the afterword to *The Four Books* I had several moments of inspiration in which I realized why I wanted to become a traitor to writing or an unfilial son of realism.

A talented young author once told me about a Chinese internet site where young people born in the 1980s and 1990s can go to express their hatred of their parents. Visitors to this site behave like spiritual criminals who have suddenly been released from their moral shackles, and they join together in cursing their parents—recounting their heinous qualities and denouncing their despicable behavior. In sum, visitors to this site can liberate themselves from their filial constraints and attack their parents as they would their most despised enemy. Even a shockingly unfilial statement like "I truly want to murder my parents" would receive resounding support in this forum, as though the speaker were giving voice to the desires of an entire generation.

I was shocked by the young author's description, but I didn't have the slightest doubt that what he said was true. Now, when addressing realism, I would echo that site's parricidal impulses. Indeed, with respect to realism—and specifically with respect to the realism we find in contemporary Chinese literature—I resemble that young person who entered the internet site and exclaimed, "I truly want to murder my parents!"

I am, indeed, an unfilial son of realism. I find it disconcerting to realize that my resistance to and hatred of realism has reached such a point—like a criminal who is preparing to carry out an assault but who finds that his conscience has not yet been fully numbed. A criminal's greatest enemy is not his actual opponent but rather his own conscience, and when I am cursing various sorts of realisms, what pains me the most is my realization that I cannot completely separate myself from them, much less kill them off. I can't simply put them to death and continue on my way. I'm like an unfilial son who, when holding a blade up to his parents' throats, suddenly remembers the hard work with which they raised and nurtured him—even though this recollection is not enough to make him put down his knife. Similarly, this unfilial rebel ultimately has no option but to flee to a remote literary wasteland, where he may remain independent and silent.

2   STRUCTURED TRUTH

When *Robinson Crusoe* was released to the world in 1719, Daniel Defoe had no way of knowing he was in the process of helping establish two of the cornerstones of literary realism: namely, experience and reality. Experience is the fertile soil out of which realism sprouts, and it is imperative that every reader share the same feelings, with the tacit understanding that authors and readers will thereby share the same experiences. Meanwhile, an author's objective, truth, is the product of this fertile soil. Experience is used by authors to reliably transmit to readers, while also functioning as the index by which authors receive recognition from those same readers. Truth is the currency of authors who practice realism, and the more truth an author possesses, the more he will be able to engage readers in a process of transfer and exchange. It is truth, not experience, that constitutes an author's figurative wealth, and to construct his own truth—which is to say, his repository of wealth—and to acquire cultural capital, an author may use a variety of different methods and elements, including fictional characters, settings, stories, plots, and psychological development, to create a realistic landscape and achieve the incomparable glory of truth.

Of course, on the path to truth, authors and readers work together to plot characters—and this is their most important contract. This contract dictates not only how an author produces a work but also how readers receive it. This is similar to how, when people first created money, they knew that exchange was the key objective and money was merely a way of making that exchange more convenient; but later, after they realized that money could be used to achieve all objectives, they came to view money as an objective in its own right. Counterfeit currency therefore came into being and became increasingly ubiquitous. Just as real money had to be continually redesigned to prevent the circulation of counterfeit currency, similarly truth, within the context of realism, continually has to advance.

At this point, we can identify four different levels of truth and their corresponding modes of realism:

1   Societally structured truth—structured realism;
2   Worldly experienced truth—worldly realism;
3   Life-experienced truth—vital realism;
4   Spiritual-depth truth—spiritual realism.

When truth becomes the kernel of realistic writing, it acquires this four-layered structure, and it is within these four levels that authors pursuing realism may dance and sing, wander and grieve. Some authors sing empty songs on the first level, to gain the confidence of their readers, while others descend to the second level, where they assume a more solemn demeanor—like an actor who climbs down from the stage to shake hands with the audience. In this way, the latter authors will make the ignorant masses feel moved and tearful. The kind of structured truth that is choreographed at the first level—which is to say, the truth of structured realism—develops primarily in centralized states and under strong ideological systems. Power and centralization are so threatening, and ideology is so strong, that structured realism and structured truth may become vast and crude. It was certainly not the case that Germany under Hitler did not have any literature and art, but rather that after the end of the fascist regime this kind of crude art took a curtain call and exited from the stage's first level. Moreover, what was departing was not only structured realism, but also a certain kind of structured truth.

Consider, for example, Erwin Kolbenheyer and Joseph Goebbels. Kolbenheyer's historical novel *Paracelsus* was regarded as a masterpiece of the Third Reich, while Goebbels's novel *Michael: A German Destiny in Diary Form* used a literary form to present the distinguishing features of Nazism and fascism, at the time attracting the interest of many fanatical youth. However, no one mentions these authors' works anymore, and they have become figurative mummies within the ranks of German literary history, to be unearthed by researchers. During the Soviet era, the transformation of Russian literature also yielded many structured-realist authors and works. After the liberation of the Soviet Union, for instance, Viktor Jerofejev argued in his influential essay "Mourning Soviet Literature" that "the tower of Soviet socialist realist literature was erected on the Stalin-Gorky plan. It featured a baroque style, and included works by Aleksey Tolstoy, Alexander Fadeyev, Pyotr Pavlenko, Fyodor Gladkov, Yegor Gaidar, and others. Although these works certainly included some inferior products, the resulting literary tower has resisted the wind and rain for decades, and has even come to influence the culture of other countries in the socialist camp."[2]

This passage reveals two secrets pertaining to the origins of structured realism and structured truth, which is to say power, and how this literature influenced the cultural production of other countries in the socialist camp. Of course, Jerofejev himself did not pursue these questions, though Chinese authors and readers take the answers to be self-evident, and we all know very well the source of the river from which we drink.

It is clear that the word *structured*, here, carries connotations of "controlled subscription and fiction." *Control* involves the use of power to impose, oppress, and coerce, while a *subscription* is a transaction that takes place after power places an order and where the author's payment is precisely the loss of their conscience and integrity—whereby authors use their personal signature to enter a mutually beneficial system of exchange. In the resulting exchange, however, the commodity remains invisible. Both sides struggle to create fiction out of nothing, to expand from experience, and to use an individual case as a broadly disseminated literary truth that either virtually doesn't exist at all or else exists only for a brief moment in time. This kind of fictional truth is the kernel and the condition of structured realism's existence and believability. Within our own 9,600,000-square-kilometer territory, this kind of literature has existed for over half a century and has developed deep roots, lush leaves, and succulent fruits. No one would doubt its existence, the same way that everyone believes in the existence of a legendary city under the sea—and while you may never have seen this legendary city with your own eyes, you nevertheless firmly believe that this is an illusory truth that virtually exists. Similarly, because our nation needs structured realism, structured truth therefore becomes the foundation on which this kind of realism rests. Over time, authors and readers have come to believe in the existence of this kind of truth, and it thereby becomes the imperative that drives the existence, thought, writing, and careers of several generations of authors.

Through a variety of literary efforts, institutions such as China's propaganda system and the Chinese Writers' Association have succeeded in constructing a system of structured realism. Their method involves the creation of an illusory truth within literature, and their objective is to make the structure appear dazzling, as though it has a universal existence, and prominent, as though it would be the fault of the era and of actual social reality if this structure were to fail to become the basis of the corresponding national literature.

George Orwell's *1984* offers a satirical commentary on every system of structured truth around the world. In artistic terms *Animal Farm* is superior to *1984*, though the prestige of the latter work has enabled it to supersede the former—because structured reality appears not only in regions dominated by ideology but also in regions dominated by power. Meanwhile, power's prevalence in the world is like people's reliance on air and water. Similarly, the existence of structured realism/truth lies precisely in its perfect intersection with power, just as its truth lies in the ubiquity of its illusoriness. If we wish to topple this tower that structured reality has constructed out of thin air, we must contend not only with power and social awareness, but also with the legions of readers and authors who have been cultivated by these works. The vast number of readers who support the existence of structured realism resembles the millions of people who supported the execution of Galileo for embracing the truth.

Fortunately, in China contemporary authors write on behalf not only of structured truth but also of worldly truth, vital truth, and spiritual truth. Some authors seeking power and fame labor tirelessly on behalf of structured truth, while others, positioned in the solitude of their private studies, struggle on behalf of worldly truth, vital truth, and spiritual-depth truth. This is one of the reasons why literature enjoys a higher stature in contemporary China than cinema, television, and the theatrical arts.

In *Gone with the Wind*, Scarlett O'Hara initially loved Ashley Wilkes, but she was ill-fated, and even after three marriages she never managed to be with a man she truly loved. Moreover, after she finally realized that her true love was not Wilkes but rather Rhett Butler, Butler abruptly left her. This love story helped *Gone with the Wind* become a classic within the worldly-realist tradition. When we describe Margaret Mitchell's novel as a classic, it is not only because the work—which was completed in 1926 and published in 1936—became a global bestseller and was made into an Oscar-winning blockbuster movie, but more importantly it is because Mitchell set the novel during the American Civil War and used the work to convey her reverence for literature. Had it not been for these latter two points, Mitchell would not have been a practitioner of worldly realism, and instead would have been merely a secular or even a vulgar realist. In a global context, worldly realism is one of the types of realism that has been most favorably received—in part because it is safest and most likely to succeed. Its danger, however, lies in the fact that there is only a slender boundary separating worldly realism from vulgar realism, and writers frequently cross back and forth between the two. Vulgar realism pursues a truth grounded in an identity associated with a specific class or group, while worldly realism aspires for a secular identity that can appeal to a broader audience. If audiences did not identify with this worldly reality, then the core of worldly reality would not exist.

Following Margaret Mitchell's success in the first half of the twentieth century, William Somerset Maugham similarly avoided the dangers of vulgar realism. Maugham's works contained stories that audiences wanted to hear, but what rendered them truly extraordinary was the way he combined a judicious use of language with ingenious humor. Meanwhile, Maugham's characters and plots were primarily selected from anecdotes about prominent actors, authors, and artists—and in this way he easily satisfied worldly realism's demand for worldly truth. His readers, accordingly, did not have to look very hard to find a comprehensible causal logic. Just as the artist in Maugham's *The Moon and Sixpence* was partially based on Paul Gaugin, the writer in *Cakes and Ale* was partially based on Thomas Hardy, and the actress in *Theatre* was a based on a composite of various actresses Maugham had known, many of Maugham's other works were similarly inspired by real figures who were then transformed into fictional characters whom readers could readily accept.

In many respects, Mitchell's and Maugham's works—including the plots, characters, cultural backgrounds, and national settings—are quite different from one another. If we consider only their respective modes of presentation, for instance, we find that one uses tragedy while the other resorts to comedy. When it comes to worldly realism's ability to transcend vulgar truth and achieve a worldly truth, however, these two authors are truly on the same page.

More generally, we may offer the following four postulates about the four different regimes of truth:

> Structured or vulgar truth rejects thought and depth.
> Worldly truth mimics thought and depth.
> Vital truth pursues thought and depth.
> Spiritual truth completes thought and depth.

In its ability to mimic thought and depth, worldly truth bears many similarities to structured truth, with the primary difference between the two being that the latter is established on a foundation of mutual unconsciousness while the former relies on a foundation of shared experience. The realism of worldly truth relies primarily on a shared experience of secular society, and its incorporation of this shared experience reinforces readers' sense of identification and approbation. To represent this shared experience, authors skillfully take social customs that virtually everyone has either personally experienced or for which they have a strong curiosity, and use them as the raw materials on which to base their fiction. If we ignore the historical period or cultural background of his works and instead merely consider the texts themselves, then Honoré de Balzac is most exemplary in this regard. If Balzac wants to function as a Parisian clerk, he has no choice but to present a detailed description and representation of the secular customs of contemporary Parisians, like an artist painting an oil painting. To transcend worldly truth and begin to approach—or perhaps even attain—a deeper life truth, Balzac's works have no choice but to treat worldly truth as the pigments with which he figuratively paints his literary works. In writing worldly truth, social customs are Balzac's charm and intention. Of course, calling Balzac a worldly realist is absurdly disrespectful, given that it was he who led us beyond worldly truth to observe—and even personally experience—the brilliance of vital truth. However, when we peruse his works themselves, we do indeed observe a large number of textual traces of worldly truths in the worldly-realist tradition, which leads us to appreciate the existence of worldly realism in his works.

With respect to their representation of the world and secular customs, Chinese authors whose writing style could be compared to Balzac's include Shen Congwen and Eileen Chang. If we consider their respective oeuvres, both latter authors have undoubtedly transcended worldly realism and approached—or even attained—a level of vital truth. However, neither of them has any qualms about using worldly and secular truth to try to win readers' respect. The success of Shen Congwen's *Border Town*, for instance, lies precisely in the author's deliberate avoidance of the complexity and depth of social reality, thereby making the avoidance of reflection a kind of reflection in its own right—the same way that Tao Yuanming's fable "Peach Blossom Spring" was Tao's response to the hard realities of war and political conflict.

Shen Congwen's *Border Town* is filled with heartfelt praise for the disappearing customs of Xiangxi Province, and because of the encroachment of the turbulent world and modern society, literature's preservation of these lost customs accords perfectly with readers' own nostalgic aesthetics, which helps explain the conjunction of *Border Town*'s aesthetics and those of multiple generations of readers. In one passage, for instance, Shen describes how,

> because of Border Town's simple customs, sex work remained a very lively occupation. When prostitutes met an unfamiliar customer, they would require that payment be made before any business was conducted, and only after counting the money carefully would they close the door and begin doing their thing. After they have gotten to know someone, however, money would fall into a space between being necessary and not necessary. These prostitutes relied primarily on Sichuan businessmen to make a living, but their true feelings actually lay with the sailors. For those with whom they feel affectionate, after they agree to separate neither side can act up.[3]

This sort of lower-class beauty is virtually nowhere to be found in today's commercial society. However, these sorts of human affairs that no longer exist can make us even more nostalgic for the remote territory that Shen Congwen describes in such loving detail. This is one of the reasons why, even today, Shen's novel still invokes a strong feeling a nostalgia. Of course, something else that cannot be underestimated is the beauty and poetic quality of the novel's use of Chinese. Even if one were to ignore the work's plot and characters, and instead simply open it to random page and begin reading, the language would give you a feeling like aged wine.

Like Shen Congwen's *Border Town*, Eileen Chang's "Shutdown," *Love in a Fallen City*, and *Red Rose White Rose* abandon the possibility of progressing further in the direction of vital truth and instead enthusiastically devote themselves to worldly secular truth. However, this simply illustrates the point that within the Chinese literary tradition, for most readers and critics worldly truth is in no way inferior to vital truth. We not only have the vital truth of vital realism exemplified by Cao Xueqin's great Qing dynasty novel, *Dream of the Red Chamber*, we also have the worldly truth of the worldly-realist tradition exemplified by the Ming dynasty novel *Plum in the Golden Vase*. Even more important is the existence and flourishing within our culture of structured truth, which grants worldly truth a reactive strength with respect to the illusory truth of structured realism. As a result, worldly realism comes to acquire its own distinctive significance and fate.

Another representative worldly-realist work is Qian Zhongshu's *Fortress Besieged*, which has been celebrated precisely for its rejection of structured realism. However, the worldly truth presented in *Fortress Besieged* is different from what we find in Eileen Chang's and Shen Congwen's works, in that whereas Chang wrote primarily about urban life and Shen Congwen's *Border Town* is a classic depiction of folk customs, *Fortress Besieged* instead focuses on the social world. The folk world has its own independent and self-contained literary sphere, while society, the nation, and the world function as the endless border of its characters and activities. Just as the folk world uses folk culture to describe individuals and regional life, the social world uses social background and social culture to describe the appearance and fate of individuals embroiled in social struggle. Despite these differences, however, both narrative modes fall under the tradition of worldly realism.

In the nineteenth century, the differences between Balzac's and Victor Hugo's purview can be found not only in the realism and romanticism of their respective novels but also in their differing attitudes toward the relationship between society and humanity. Balzac's works treated people and society as chaotically intertwined, while Hugo's viewed them as separate and irreconcilable. The former are praised as critical realism, while the latter are regarded as romantic realism. Most of the characters in the former play roles in society or the folk world, while those in the latter are often positioned in theatrical society and on a religious stage. The truth of the folk world is largely reliant on the truth of life experience, and regardless of whether this truth is critical or laudatory, it is fundamentally ambiguous. However, this kind of truth either matches readers' own experience or else is an experience with which they can readily identify. Meanwhile, social truth does not accord with the personal experience of most readers and instead is merely something they dream about or yearn for. Balzac's characters seem to be right next to us, while Hugo's exist only in our imagination. Moreover, the kind of reading experience I describe here is not unique to Chinese authors and readers; I suspect that everyone who loves nineteenth-century fiction would have a similar response.

Returning to the topic of Chinese literature's worldly truth, *Border Town* is a prototypical example of a work that presents a rural worldly truth, and Eileen Chang exemplifies an urban worldly truth, while *Fortress Besieged* focuses on the social world. With respect to the writings of Ba Jin, meanwhile, the contemporary Chinese literary critic Chen Sihe has observed:

> When we look back at Ba Jin's life—from his early status as an activist with a belief in society, to being a very accomplished and famous author, to being someone who, in his later years, was a social conscience who wrote numerous "Random Thought" essays reflecting on the concept of revolution—we see that beginning with social movements and concluding with social criticism, Ba Jin's greatest concern was always how Chinese society could develop in a healthy manner, and how the Chinese people could live reasonably. Accordingly, it would not be an exaggeration to use the phrase "worrying about the nation and its people" to describe Ba Jin's life.[4]

This passage captures the dedication and effort with which Ba Jin approached the task of writing about the social world, while the works of Lao She represent an amalgam of the social and folk worlds. It is difficult to say who was more mature, Ba Jin or Lao She, just as it is impossible to say who is greater, Balzac or Hugo. The difference between Ba Jin and Lao She lies not in the degree to which they divide and intermix the social and folk worlds, but rather in whose work is most able to transcend the world and attain, like Balzac's and Hugo's novels, the deeper realm of life reality.

In China's hermeneutical and critical tradition, the writing of the truth of the social world falls under the category of "rapid-cooking" works, which is why Chinese authors always flock toward this mode of writing. Meanwhile, the reality of the folk world falls under the category of "slow-cooking" works, which is why the ranks of these authors are relatively small, though latecomers invariably get the upper hand. The reason for this is that novels about the folk world remain relatively stable over time, while those about the social world are often unstable, given that society itself undergoes countless transformations. This may remind people of the worldly writings of Margaret Mitchell and Somerset Maugham, in that Mitchell had a broad social background, in contrast to Chinese realistic authors whose writings previously were regarded as classics but who subsequently progressed toward desolate, fated social realism, like retired cadre authors, while Maugham rejected broad historical settings, which is also different from what we find in Chinese folk literature. If Mitchell and Maugham had been Chinese and if their works had taken the form of Chinese worldly realism, it is unclear how literary critics and historians might have perceived them. In fact, I often wonder if Scarlett O'Hara had been born in China, if Margaret Mitchell had been like Eileen Chang, and if the plot of *Gone with the Wind* had unfolded against the backdrop of either China's early twentieth-century warlord period, the Long March, the War of Resistance against Japan, or the Chinese Civil War, then how would we have received this Chinese version of Mitchell's novel, and how would we have regarded its counterfactual Chinese author? Would we still have viewed it as a literary classic?

If we view worldly truth as realism's dance on the second level of truth, then its strength naturally derives from its efforts to reach the third level—which is to say, vital truth. Vital truth is the objective of all ambitious authors, and particularly of those who practice realism. Balzac and Hugo were model examples, while in China, Lu Xun is the author who can be most easily included in these ranks. Although Lu Xun never produced a magnum opus like Gustave Flaubert's *Madame Bovary*, Stendhal's *The Red and the Black*, or Hugo's *Les Misérables*, he was nevertheless a pioneer in the quest for vital truth.

When twentieth-century critics looked back at the leaders of nineteenth-century realism—whether it be Balzac following a worldly path or Hugo following a social drama path—they observed that these earlier authors sought a deep level of realism to create a vital truth. In this respect, Leo Tolstoy's calm display of vital truth is even more admirable than that of other realist masters. Why is this? It is because all the realist authors who managed to attain a level of vital truth shared a basic rule or, we might say, a common constraint: fictional characters must be perfectly matched with the era in which they are positioned, such that the most representative characters help to construct their corresponding era. The more perfectly that representative fictional characters are matched with their historical era, the more likely it is that a work will achieve a canonical status. This is a rule that has been collectively established by authors, readers, and critics, and it requires that authors function as the spiritual practitioners and regulators of their era. Authors must have a complete mastery of the era's spirit, and only in this way will they be able to create fictional characters who are perfectly matched with that era. This is like an enormous tree that emerges from a plot of fertile soil, or a towering peak that rises up out of a chain of mountains—because otherwise the fertile soil would lose its meaning and the mountain will become merely a string of flat hills.

It is impossible to imagine realistic fiction without representative characters. When we think of *Don Quixote*—the anti-chivalric novel Miguel de Cervantes wrote 115 years before Defoe's *Robinson Crusoe*—it is virtually impossible to imagine that the work could have had much significance for the future development of realism had it lacked the iconic protagonists Don Quixote and Sancho Panza. Similarly, Daniel Defoe's status as an author relies on Robinson Crusoe's existence as a character. When realistic fiction takes truth as its most important responsibility, fictional characters become the most powerful evidence for the existence of this truth. Therefore, the transition from worldly truth to vital truth is predicated on a concurrent transition from worldly characters to vital characters.

Over the course of realism's development, characters have progressed from worldly truth to vital truth. For instance, Balzac's novels *Le Père Goriot* and *Eugénie Grandet* have become models of works where the folk world and the social world are in perfect harmony, thereby helping establish a trajectory through which representative characters may progress from worldly truth to vital truth. Many later authors followed in Balzac's footsteps, and sometimes they even managed to surpass him—creating fictional characters who were capable of standing in for the authors themselves.

Many great works from the nineteenth century are named after their protagonists (or objects related to their protagonists), joining a long tradition that includes works such as François Rabelais's *Gargantua and Pantagruel*, *Don Quixote*, Johann Wolfgang von Goethe's *Faust* and *The Sorrows of Young Werther*, Henry Fielding's *The History of Tom Jones*, *Robinson Crusoe*, Charlotte Brontë's *Jane Eyre*, Charles Dickens's *The Pickwick Papers*, John Galsworthy's *The Forsyte Saga*, *Le Père Goriot*, *Eugénie Grandet*, *Madame Bovary*, Hardy's *Tess of the d'Ubervilles*, Tolstoy's *Anna Karenina*, Ivan Turgenev's *Fathers and Sons*, Fyodor Dostoevsky's *The Brothers Karamazov*, Jack London's *Martin Eden*, and Lu Xun's *The True Story of Ah Q*. All these works are evidence of the paramount status of characters within the realist tradition. Because the vital truth that is realism's objective involves the reality and depth of people's lives, it is therefore natural that representative characters would become a powerful fulcrum with which the author's pen would be able to lift up the world of vital truth.

If a nineteenth-century realist author had failed to create a distinctive protagonist, we would likely have no choice but to exclude him from the pantheon of great authors. For instance, if Tolstoy had not created characters like Anna Karenina and Katyusha Maslova, we would be unable to consider him a great author, much less view him as a dazzling light within this elite group. Without the two protagonists who anchor *Anna Karenina* and *Resurrection*, the realism of these works would have collapsed. Similarly, we could ask whether it is thanks to Flaubert that Emma Bovary has become immortal, or is it instead thanks to Emma Bovary that Flaubert will live forever in our hearts. Balzac's novels *Le Père Goriot* and *Eugénie Grandet* perfectly meld the households they describe with nineteenth-century French moneyed society, granting these works a complementary significance. The works' protagonists are enslaved by money, but they nevertheless helped make Balzac rich and powerful, granting him an undisputed position within the ranks of realist authors. We could also consider Hugo's Jean Valjean and Quasimodo; Stendhal's Julien and Fabris; Anton Chekhov's Ochumelov in "Chameleon," Chervyakov in "Civil Servants," and Olga Ivanovna in "The Jumping Woman"; or Guy de Maupassant's Mathilde Loisel in "The Necklace" and the prostitute Elisabeth Rousset, also known as Butterball, in "Butterball." If these authors had not given us such true, full, and distinctive characters, our respect for them would have been significantly diminished.

The brilliance of the great nineteenth-century authors derives from the degree to which their fiction can analyze the depth of their corresponding era and the richness and complexity of their fictional characters. These are the two legs on which their greatness rests. However, as the gap between the historical era of the authors and that of their later readers increases, readers' evaluation of these authors comes to rely more and more on their works' fictional characters, while the works' historical background becomes a concern primarily for academics. Meanwhile, the more that fictional characters are viewed as actual individuals, the more brilliant their authors will be perceived to be. A character's vital truth becomes a key metric for assessing an author's brilliance.

Tolstoy and Turgenev were contemporaries, though they maintained a distance from one another and never ended up meeting in person. In that great age of social transformation, they stood together at the forefront of Russian literature, to the point that in some respects Turgenev even surpassed Tolstoy. When Turgenev published *Fathers and Sons* in 1862, for instance, the protagonists Yevgény Vasílevich Bazárov and Pável Petróvich Kirsánov attracted considerable interest among society's leftists and rightists, and even incited a series of protests and arson attacks in Saint Petersburg that lasted more than a year. As J. M. Coetzee later notes, "In Russian literary history, and even world literary history, there is no other author who has been the object of such fierce and prolonged attacks from both leftists and rightists."[5] From this, we can readily imagine that Turgenev's popularity during that period must have been as great as the sun in the middle of the sky. Today, however—and especially for Chinese readers and critics—Tolstoy's *War and Peace*, *Anna Karenina*, and *Resurrection* enjoy significantly greater acclaim than Turgenev's *Rudin*, *On the Eve*, *Fathers and Sons*, *Virgin Soil*, and *A Sportsman's Sketches*. Why is this? It is because Tolstoy's works are more resilient than Turgenev's when it comes to the link between characters and their corresponding era. The former placed more emphasis on "humanity" and human life, while the latter placed more emphasis on "social individuals" and the process of social differentiation to which those individuals are subjected. As the translator's note to the Chinese edition of *Anna Karenina* observes, Tolstoy felt that some observers futilely imagine people as being either strong or weak, good or evil, smart or stupid. In reality, however, everyone has aspects of both: sometimes people are strong, and sometimes they are weak; sometimes they are rational, and sometimes they are confused; sometimes they are good, and sometimes they are bad. People are not a fixed constant, but rather they are constantly changing—sometimes falling and sometimes rising.

Because of Tolstoy's complex understanding of people's life processes, Anna Karenina was presented as "a marvelous, sweet and unhappy woman," and even as she was contemplating suicide, she still managed to observe "a misshapen lady wearing a bustle (Anna mentally undressed the woman and was appalled at her hideousness)."[6] This sort of description elevates Anna's realism, and her vital truth, to a terrifying level.

Just before Anna commits suicide, meanwhile, she reflects,

> Yes, I am very troubled, and reason was given man that he might escape his troubles. Therefore I must escape. Why not put out the candle where there's nothing more to see, when everything looks obnoxious? But how? Why did that guard run along the footboard? Why do those young men in the next carriage make such a noise? Why do they talk and laugh? Everything is false and evil—all lies and deceit![7]

Almost all commentators cite this passage when discussing Anna's cry to the world, but we might also compare the scene in which Anna throws herself under the train:

> And exactly at the moment when the space between the wheels drew level with her she threw aside the red bag and drawing her head down between her shoulders dropped on her hands under the truck, and with a light movement, as though she would rise again at once, sank on to her knees. At that same instant she became horror-struck at what she was doing. "Where am I What am I doing? Why?" She tried to get up, to throw herself back; but something huge and relentless struck her on the head and dragged her down on her back. "God forgive me everything!" she murmured, feeling the impossibility of struggling. A little peasant muttering something was working at the rails. And the candle by which she had been reading the book filled with trouble and deceit, sorrow and evil, flared up with a brighter light, illuminating for her everything that before had been enshrouded in darkness, flickered, grew dim and went out for ever.[8]

On the surface, this appears to be merely a description of Anna's death, but in reality it offers a meticulous description of the depth of a fictional character's vital truth.

From the protagonist of *Anna Karenina* we can discern humanity's vital essence, and from Bazarov in *Sons and Lovers* we can discern the political orientation of his social consciousness. This is the key difference between Tolstoy and Turgenev, and it is also the key difference between how we perceive their works today—more than a century after they stood together at the forefront of their era's literary realism.

We could also consider Stendhal's *The Red and the Black* along similar lines. The author himself describes his novel as "a record of the year 1830," though from our contemporary perspective the work's broad social panorama and its analysis of early nineteenth-century French bourgeois social order appear rather cumbersome. Nevertheless, the novel still leaves us with lasting memories thanks to the richness, complexity, and uniqueness of the protagonist Julien Sorel, which truly marks the expansion of vital truth. When we, as contemporary readers, encounter canonical realist works, our expectation is that the realism of a character's life may exceed the work's ability to reveal a complex social reality, and the character may thereby transcend his or her corresponding historical period and come to assume a universal significance for all humanity.

It has already been nearly a century since Lu Xun published *The True Story of Ah Q*. Why does the work's iconic protagonist still enjoy such a full-bodied existence in the heart of every Chinese reader? It is because Ah Q, as a character, effectively transcended his complex social background and historical era, and has come to acquire a universal significance that is relevant to readers today. This is one of Lu Xun's most representative creations, and one that is most replete with vital truth. Were it not for this and other works filled with characters' lives, we would find ourselves truly tongue-tied when considering whether to include Lu Xun among the world's great authors. Of course, it is our eternal regret that China has not produced any full-length novels that could be included in the ranks of the immortal realist novels that manage to re-create a broad historical era with complex characters. However, we are still filled with pride when we note that in the early twentieth-century period, Chinese authors kept pace with world literature.

For instance, like Lu Xun, Maupassant was a master of the short story, and although it is true that he also produced novels such as *A Life* and *Bel Ami*, readers have generally ignored these latter works, and some have even wondered why Balzac needed to write them in the first place. "Butterball," meanwhile, was only ten thousand characters long (in Chinese translation), but its analysis of people and society rivalled that of a three-hundred-thousand-character novel like *A Life*. Accordingly, we need not lament the fact that Lu Xun never produced a great realist novel, since even if he had, who could guarantee that it would have been comparable to the great novels of the nineteenth century? Instead, with his short story collections *Call to Arms* and *Hesitation*, Lu Xun became the first Chinese author to reach the level of vital truth, and perhaps this is already sufficient for us to be proud of our realism. What we should regret, however, is that our later realist authors did not follow this path in the direction of a vital truth that is even more distant, broader, and deeper than realism. Instead, revolution ended up leading literature around by the nose, and literature reverted from vital truth back to worldly truth, or even further back to structured truth. Furthermore, after several decades, it was difficult to break free from this process—like an ox or mule being led around in circles as it turns a grindstone.

In his *History of Modern Chinese Fiction*, the venerable C. T. Hsia used his Chinese and Western scholarly training and his unique understanding of Chinese literature to critique the long-standing bias, within Chinese literary histories, toward the sort of social truth found in worldly novels—allowing Hsia to elevate folk realist authors like Shen Congwen and Eileen Chang, as well as novels like Qian Zhongshu's *Fortress Besieged*. This constituted a welcome correction to literary history's deviations, thereby returning Chinese literary history to the correct path. Shen Congwen's subsequent canonization was due in large part to the vital truth that permeates his writings, together with his resistance to the influence of worldly and social truth. Meanwhile, the current popularity of Eileen Chang's worldly reality is similarly due to readers' dissatisfaction with China's powerful regime of structured realism. The act of reading and enjoying Eileen Chang's works may be seen as a gesture of resistance to a ubiquitous structured realism and its corresponding structured truth. What is surprising, however, is that C. T. Hsia devoted no attention to Xiao Hong, whose works exemplified a form of vital truth, and as a result his literary history's objectivity was fundamentally compromised.

We normally don't permit critics to set aside their objectivity and critique literature in an emotional manner, though we do allow authors to express themselves in this way. Accordingly, if I were to rely on my personal preferences to understand the status of realism in modern Chinese literary history from the perspective of worldly truth and vital truth, I would focus on Xiao Hong, as well as on figures like Lu Xun, Shen Congwen, Lao She, Eileen Chang, Ba Jin, Yu Dafu, and Mao Dun.

5   SPIRITUAL-DEPTH TRUTH

In an essay on Dostoevsky, J. M. Coetzee cites Joseph Frank's five-volume literary biography and concludes that

> at the risk of exaggeration, Frank calls Dostoevsky "a literary proletarian forced to write for wages" (343). About the circumstances that kept him on the literary treadmill Dostoevsky felt considerable bitterness. Even

with *Crime and Punishment*—an enormous popular success—and *The Idiot* behind him, he felt a painful sense of inferiority to Turgenev and Tolstoy, both held in higher critical esteem (and paid more per page) than he. He envied these rivals their time and leisure and inherited fortunes; he looked forward to the day when he would be able to tackle a truly major theme and prove himself their equal. He sketched in some detail an ambitious work, called first *Atheism*, then *The Life of a Great Sinner*, intended to bring him recognition as a serious writer. But these sketches had to be cannibalized for *The Devils*, and the major opus was again postponed.[9]

This interesting description reveals that Dostoevsky felt inferior to Turgenev and Tolstoy because he had not yet written a novel about "a truly major theme." Coetzee suggests that Dostoevsky yearned for the day when he would be able to write such a work and thereby become a "serious writer." Regardless of whether we are examining nineteenth-century Russian golden age literature or browsing the works of Russia's great critical realist authors, we may observe that these works all strive to analyze and reveal the complexity and changes of their era. These works originated from and developed against a broad social background, and otherwise it would have been difficult for them to have entered the ranks of greatness or for their authors to be considered serious writers.

The representative characters that appear in works by canonical realist authors are definitely complex social products. Dostoevsky, however, was not that kind of author, and although his novels did have a strong correspondence with the realities of nineteenth-century Russian society, they didn't feature the same sort of broad social background that we find in works such as Tolstoy's *War and Peace* and Turgenev's *Fathers and Sons*. A complex social background is the foundation in which realist novels are grounded, and is the explosive buried behind the grand narrative from which realism derives its power. This is what Dostoevsky had in mind when he aspired to be recognized as a serious writer and to write a novel on a truly major theme. This particular quality, however, is precisely what he lacked, which made him feel deeply frustrated. What Dostoevsky did not anticipate, however, was that his fiction would end up providing a template for the next level of realism—namely, spiritual-depth realism, which offered an even richer and more creative model for representing reality. In this way, his writings offered a bridge to the earth-shattering transformations that literature would undergo in the twentieth century. In other words, his novels opened the door for the twentieth-century modern novel.

Spiritual-depth truth is the highest level of truth in realist fiction, and is erected on the foundation of realism's search for a new truth superseding vital truth. Many nineteenth-century literary masters transitioned from vital truth to spiritual-depth truth, but it is difficult to find a figure like Dostoevsky, who from the first to the last page of every work consistently depicted humanity's spiritual depth and enabled his characters' spirit produce a dazzling light of truth. Yue Lin's early translations allowed Chinese readers to realize that spiritual-depth truth was Dostoevsky's great foundation, and also the apex of realism's truth. Furthermore, this kind of spiritual truth was the product not of a single plotline or a single story but rather of an entire novel, or even multiple novels—it was a product of a great author's entire oeuvre. For instance, Yue Lin's preface to *Crime and Punishment* describes how

> Dostoevsky was born into lower society and was therefore very familiar with the lives of poor people in dirty allies and dank rooms, and he had a deep sympathy for their fate. It was precisely because he had such a strong sense of sympathy for the social underclass that he was therefore able to write deeply and movingly about tragedy, suffering, and humiliation, thereby placing his readers into an atmosphere of acute sorrow and inciting their anger and hatred toward the capitalist system. He was the first nineteenth-century Russian author to write about the suffering of the urban poor, and he became a spokesperson for Russia's poor urban class.[10]

This is a very "Chinese" understanding of the author, and even today it continues to distort many Chinese readers' appreciation of realism. Sigmund Freud, meanwhile, was fond of Dostoevsky's work, calling *The Brothers Karamazov* the most magnificent novel to date, but he was approaching this work from the perspective of psychoanalysis and not from the perspective of the characters' souls. However, if we approach Dostoevsky's novels from the perspective of realism's soul—which is to say, from the deepest level of reality—there is no doubt that they advance realism to a level of spiritual truth that transcends vital truth. Dostoevsky took realism to the final level, and in this way was able to grant it a final punctuation mark. As a result, he ensured that twentieth-century novels would have no choice but to start over again.

In attaining spiritual truth, realism began to slip from its earlier pinnacle—though it is unclear whether this was realism's good fortune or was instead an elegy for a kind of truth through which realistic literature must inevitably pass. In any event, when Dostoevsky performed his elegy for the truth found in realist fiction, he covered literature's path with an array of behaviors, shouts, and convulsions associated with spiritual truth. In *Crime and Punishment*, for example, we clearly see the depiction of Raskolnikov's soul, which begins with his inner convulsions when he finds himself avoiding his landlady because he is unable to pay his rent:

> For some time past he had been in an overstrained irritable condition, verging on hypochondria. He had become so completely absorbed in himself, and isolated from his fellows that he dreaded meeting, not only his landlady, but anyone at all. He was crushed by poverty, but the anxieties of his position had of late ceased to weigh upon him. He had given up attending to matters of practical importance; he had lost all desire to do so.[11]

Following this initial exposition, Raskolnikov quickly progresses from being a character to being a soul:

> It was dusk when he was waked up by a fearful scream. Good God, what a scream! Such unnatural sounds, such howling, wailing, grinding, tears, blows and curses he had never heard.
>
> He could never have imagined such brutality, such frenzy. In terror he sat up in bed, almost swooning with agony. But the fighting, wailing and cursing grew louder and louder. And then to his intense amazement he caught the voice of his landlady. She was howling, shrieking and wailing, rapidly, hurriedly, incoherently, so that he could not make out what she was talking about; she was beseeching, no doubt, not to be beaten, for she was being mercilessly beaten on the stairs. The voice of her assailant was so horrible from spite and rage that it was almost a croak; but he, too, was saying something, and just as quickly and indistinctly, hurrying and spluttering. All at once Raskolnikov trembled; …
>
> Raskolnikov sank worn out on the sofa, but could not close his eyes. He lay for half an hour in such anguish, such an intolerable sensation of infinite terror as he had never experienced before.[12]

Although this might appear to be an extremely realistic description of the landlady being beaten, in reality the scene is the product of Raskolnikov's fever-induced delirium. More importantly, this delirium is a product of Raskolnikov's soul's confession after he murders the pawnbroker, and when Raskolnikov finally goes to the police station to confess, his trembling soul begins to protest and rebel:

> Then, I remember, I maintain in my article that all ... well, legislators and leaders of men, such as Lycurgus, Solon, Mahomet, Napoleon, and so on, were all without exception criminals, from the very fact that, making a new law, they transgressed the ancient one, handed down from their ancestors and held sacred by the people, and they did not stop short at bloodshed either, if that bloodshed—often of innocent persons fighting bravely in defense of ancient law—were of use to their cause. It's remarkable, in fact, that the majority, indeed, of these benefactors and leaders of humanity were guilty of terrible carnage. In short, I maintain that all great men or even men a little out of the common, that is to say capable of giving some new word, must from their very nature be criminals—more or less, of course.... As for my division of people into ordinary and extraordinary, I acknowledge that it's somewhat arbitrary, but I don't insist upon exact numbers. I only believe in my leading idea that men are in general divided by a law of nature into two categories, inferior (ordinary), that is, so to say, material that serves only to reproduce its kind, and men who have the gift or the talent to utter a new word. There are, of course, innumerable sub-divisions, but the distinguishing features of both categories are fairly well marked. The first category, generally speaking, are men conservative in temperament and law-abiding; they live under control and love to be controlled.... The second category all transgress the law; they are destroyers or disposed to destruction according to their capacities.[13]

However, when Raskolnikov is faced with his beloved Sonia, he finds that his soul, which had previously attempted to refute the murder charges, suddenly undergoes a transformation and he confesses to her:

> I simply did it; I did the murder for myself, for myself alone, and whether I became a benefactor to others, or spent my life like a spider catching men in my web and sucking the life out of men, I couldn't have

cared at that moment.... And it was not the money I wanted, Sonia, when I did it. It was not so much the money I wanted, but something else.... I know it all now.... Understand me! Perhaps I should never have committed a murder again. I wanted to find out something else; it was something else led me on. I wanted to find out then and quickly whether I was a louse like everybody else or a man. Whether I can step over barriers or not, whether I dare stoop to pick up or not, whether I am a trembling creature or whether I have the right....

But how did I murder her? Is that how men do murders? Do men go to commit a murder as I went then? I will tell you some day how I went! Did I murder the old woman? I murdered myself, not her! I crushed myself once for all, forever.... But it was the devil that killed that old woman, not I.[14]

Love is great, and when religion and love are united, even a criminal soul is capable of producing a dazzling light. The law might not catch someone for their crimes, but a vital soul cannot ignore them. Everything about Raskolnikov derives from the fact that he is a criminal but also has a vital soul, and at no point does he ever stop agonizing over whether a soul is the enemy or confederate of criminality. The result is that he is unable to rest easy for even a second, until his trembling, living soul finally conquers his guilty heart:

He looked eagerly to right and left, gazed intently at every object and could not fix his attention on anything; everything slipped away. "In another week, another month I shall be driven in a prison van over this bridge, how shall I look at the canal then? I should like to remember this!" slipped into his mind. "Look at this sign! How shall I read those letters then?" ...

He suddenly recalled Sonia's words, "Go to the cross-roads, bow down to the people, kiss the earth, for you have sinned against it too, and say aloud to the whole world, 'I am a murderer.'" He trembled, remembering that. And the hopeless misery and anxiety of all that time, especially of the last hours, had weighed so heavily upon him that he positively clutched at the chance of this new unmixed, complete sensation. It came over him like a fit; it was like a single spark kindled in his soul and spreading fire through him. Everything in him softened at once and the tears started into his eyes. He fell to the earth on the spot....

He knelt down in the middle of the square, bowed down to the earth, and kissed that filthy earth with bliss and rapture. He got up and bowed down a second time....

These exclamations and remarks checked Raskolnikov, and the words, "I am a murderer," which were perhaps on the point of dropping from his lips, died away. He bore these remarks quietly, however, and, without looking round, he turned down a street leading to the police office.[15]

This former college student transitions from being a murderer to attempting to defend his actions to finally accepting his soul's judgment, and, after kissing the ground, going to the police station to turn himself in. In this way, over hundreds of pages, Raskolnikov's trembling soul is finally fully realized. Among the great realist authors of the nineteenth century, only Dostoevsky managed to achieve a kind of spiritual truth that transcends ordinary life, and most important in this respect is the way in which, in the character of Raskolnikov, Dostoevsky did not stop at the level of corporeality of a dead soul and instead allowed Raskolnikov's soul to produce a light that illuminates humanity.

Another character with a soul capable of illuminating humanity's spirit is Alyosha in *Brothers Karamazov*. Alyosha's understanding of sin and suffering is even broader and greater than Raskolnikov's, and consequently his spiritual light is even warmer and more dazzling:

[Alyosha] did not stop on the steps either, but went quickly down; his soul, overflowing with rapture, yearned for freedom, space, openness. The vault of heaven, full of soft, shining stars, stretched vast and fathomless above him. The Milky Way ran in two pale streams from the zenith to the horizon. The fresh, motionless, still night enfolded the earth. The white towers and golden domes of the cathedral gleamed out against the sapphire sky. The gorgeous autumn flowers, in the beds round the house, were slumbering till morning. The silence of earth seemed to melt into the silence of the heavens. The mystery of earth was one with the mystery of the stars....

Alyosha stood, gazed, and suddenly threw himself down on the earth. He did not know why he embraced it. He could not have told why he longed so irresistibly to kiss it, to kiss it all. But he kissed it weeping, sobbing and watering it with his tears, and vowed passionately to love it, to love it for ever and ever. "Water the earth with the tears of your joy and love those tears," echoed in his soul.[16]

The difference between having a "small soul" and a "great soul" lies in a character's ability to use spiritual-depth truth to illuminate humanity's spirit. Dostoevsky's writings produced countless characters' souls, which allowed characters like Alyosha and Raskolnikov shine with the light of a great soul. This kind of pursuit of spiritual truth allowed Dostoevsky to transcend nineteenth-century realism. When later authors faced realism's primary subject—which is to say, truth—they were like tiny blades of grass struggling to grow beneath a towering tree, and all their efforts had to go toward merely swaying back and forth beneath the great tree. This makes us realize that the transformations literature underwent in the twentieth century were not only inevitable but also the product of the imprint that nineteenth-century literature left on the twentieth century.

6 TRUTH'S INTERDEPENDENCIES

The division of truth into the levels of structured truth, worldly truth, vital truth, and spiritual-depth truth is similar to the act of chopping an object into countless fragments. However, it is only because a butcher dismembers an animal that we are thereby able to access the animal's interior—thereby permitting us to observe not only the animal's vital organs but also useless ones like its appendix. Constructed truth can be compared to the animal's appendix, worldly truth can be compared to its skin and flesh, and vital truth can be compared to its skeleton, while spiritual-depth truth can be compared to its bone marrow. It is only by virtue of these various elements that it thereby becomes possible to constitute realism's corporeal structure, including even the postsocialist constructed realism that ultimately brought literature no benefit and plenty of harm.

Of course, postsocialist Chinese literary realism is simultaneously separated from and connected to these four different levels of truth. It can easily break through the first level to borrow the second level's cosmetics and use them to conceal its own hollow interior. This is also the form that Maoist-era socialist realism took after it developed and "matured" in the postsocialist era. Chinese readers are charmingly simple, and when faced with literary truth they often behave like rural children visiting the city for the first time—and either they hate literary truth the way rural migrants hate the city, or else they love it like a child from the countryside who feels that even the city's toilets and trash bins are inexpressibly wonderful. As long as constructed reality's empty writing can borrow some cosmetics from worldly reality, this will be sufficient to make clumsy critics and rural children celebrate and cheer in the newspapers, on television, and over online media. In this way, a handful of obsequious critics and shameless media figures may collude to deceive readers, under this sort of encouragement readers may come to believe that constructed truth is life, existence, and reality, because the characters in those stories stand on their own two feet. Facing the masses whom they want to educate, these critics may utter an assortment of foul words and perform a set of profane actions. For instance, the "new hero" type of structured-realist protagonist who frequently appears in prize-winning novels and on the big screen is treated as a character straight out of a historical epic and viewed as the new "hot" one by readers, audiences, and those scholars who occasionally don their critic's cap to earn some extra money. The result is that those who benefit from this process are a select group of critics and the authors themselves, while it is precisely the hoodwinked readers who are insulted and harmed.

Constructed truth often crosses over to worldly truth, to borrow its techniques in an attempt to conceal its own emptiness, falsehood, and obsequiousness. However, even after crossing over to worldly truth, constructed truth will not be able to cross over again to the domain of vital truth. This is because worldly truth can help confirm constructed truth's "realism," while vital truth can only confirm its fictionality. This is like those people who frequently use their support of Lu Xun as evidence of their own political correctness, but who would never dream of actually adopting Lu Xun's style.

The most successful contemporary authors in the worldly-realist tradition can find abundant sustenance in the works of Zhou Zuoren, Eileen Chang, and Hu Lancheng, although they may also find themselves unable to accept the works of these same authors. Shen Congwen is another good model for contemporary authors seeking to retouch their literary ornamentation, though it is also true that many of his novels have transitioned far into the realm of vital truth. For instance, constructed truth would have trouble accepting the ethereal quality of Shen's *Border Town*. Maxim Gorky is not mentioned much by these contemporary writers, and neither is Pavel Korchagin. Whenever literature loses its source model, it can become unstable, which reflects a fundamental anxiety about constructed truth's position within literature. In any event, it would be a mistake to compare constructed truth to a balloon that is liable to pop as soon as you touch it. Instead, it is important to recognize that constructed truth is still developing, and not only is its approach to worldly truth a product of its technique, but furthermore its "artistry" is refined and perfect.

Because of worldly truth's support for the artistry of constructed truth, it can therefore enjoy power's affirmation of its canonical status and support of its artistic achievements. Eileen Chang was no exception to this rule. Within the realm of worldly truth, folk-worldly truth probably does not receive much support, while what receives the most support are those authors and works that promote socio-worldly truth. However, folk-worldly realist writing, because it neglects socio-worldly truth, is best used for folk-worldly descriptions, and in this way it may approach the truth of lower-class existence. Beautiful or ugly, good or evil—these works can approach or even enter the level of vital truth, thereby achieving a perfect union of worldly and vital truth while also being recognized by the world. Works like Shen Congwen's "Xiaoxiao," "The Husband," and *Long River*, as well as Eileen Chang's "The Golden Cangue," *Love in a Fallen City*, and *Red Rose, White Rose*, have come to come to occupy a permanent position within the canon.

Worldly fiction is the largest and strongest category within traditional Chinese fiction. For instance, Feng Menglong's *Stories from a Ming Collection* was beloved and critically acclaimed and was able to become canonized even though it does not accord with the corpus of vital truth. For many readers, Wang Zengqi's short stories "Buddhist Initiation" and "Chronicles of Danao" follow the same pattern. I personally don't think these latter two works are all that extraordinary, because they don't contain many living qualities or the feeling of flowing blood. Nevertheless, whenever I have free time, I may read a few passages from these works, like sipping a nicely aged wine. After all, the phrase *literature is the art of language* is rooted in the heart and has considerable practical value, and when it comes to linguistic artistry, Wang Zengqi's two stories certainly have many excellent qualities. In the end, however, worldly literature is not able to enter the realm of vital truth and vital reality. It can only receive popular commendation but is unable to achieve the level of greatness that leaves people truly amazed.

Among modern Chinese authors, Lu Xun was the first to elevate worldly literature to the level of vital truth, and as a result, vital truth became the direction and domain of worldly literature—which received its perfect development and expression at Lu Xun's hands. It is precisely because of his commitment to vital truth, and more specifically his drive to push vital truth in the direction of spiritual-depth truth, that Lu Xun was able to be elevated to the ranks of true greatness.

With respect to fiction's transition from vital truth to spiritual-depth truth, if we were to set up a scale with Lu Xun on one side and Tolstoy and Dostoevsky on the other, or if we were to have the soul of a character like Lu Xun's Ah Q from *The True Story of Ah Q* on one side and that of a character like Maslova from *Resurrection*, Raskolnikov from *Crime and Punishment*, or Alyosha from *The Brothers Karamazov* on the other, we would have no choice but to concede that Ah Q just might be outweighed by Maslova, Raskolnikov, or Alyosha. We therefore tend to avoid this sort of direct comparison, and if we have no choice but to discuss it, we do so with considerable trepidation. This is a reflection of our pride and vanity when it comes to realism, and also of our love and respect for Lu Xun. In truth, Lu Xun probably would not have minded if we had made these sorts of comparisons, the same way that he was not particularly concerned about the possibility of winning the Nobel Prize. Lu Xun's generosity and humility permits us to say that in spiritual-depth truth, there are great souls and small ones; some souls are heavy, and naturally there are also others that are light. Even if we are unwilling to acknowledge that some of Lu Xun's characters are but small souls (like the father Old Shuan in "Medicine," for instance), we cannot deny that characters like Maslova, Raskolnikov, and Alyosha surely rank among the great souls within realism's highest level of truth.

Liu Zaifu and his daughter Liu Jianmei reach a similar conclusion when they compare Dostoevsky to Cao Xueqin, the author of *Dream of the Red Chamber*:

> Although these two authors had very different beliefs, they each had the gentlest, kindest, and most benevolent souls. Theirs were souls that no knowledge system could match, and they were extraordinarily

sensitive, particularly when it came to human suffering. Dostoyevsky's soul was seized by suffering, as was Cao Xueqin's. The only difference between the two authors is that one leaned toward an embrace of suffering, while the other leaned toward a transcendence of suffering. The eyes of these two geniuses were always overflowing of tears, and regardless of whether these were tears of gratitude or tears of sadness, they were always full of compassionate love. Each author created a pinnacle of world literature, and although they had different styles, they both told us that regardless of what position or "ism" you happen to hold, in creating a great literary work you should possess a loving and compassionate spirit. All elegies must first of all be elegies to the great love located in the depths of the soul and emotion.[17]

When Liu Zaifu and Liu Jianmei speak of great love, they are probably referring to the weight of one's soul, which is the key difference between a small soul and a great one. However, within our belated modernism, Lu Xun already devoted his life to revealing the true writing of an author's soul, and we cannot also ask him for spiritual depth or the difference between a great and a small soul.

Regardless of whether we are considering constructed truth, worldly truth, living truth, or spiritual-depth truth, in realist writing none of these truth levels can exist independently of the others. If it were possible to remove constructed truth from discussions of realism and instead treat worldly truth, vital truth, and spiritual-depth truth as literature's highest levels, these three levels would still rely on one another. However, the fundamental appearance of these truth levels can still be meticulously distinguished. Just as worldly truth is very likely to enter vital truth, vital truth is similarly very likely to enter spiritual truth or spiritual-depth truth. Whereas worldly-realist works permit us to appreciate the author's writing, they may also transition from vital truth to spiritual-depth truth—as is the case with some works by Shen Congwen and Eileen Chang. In the end, however, we cannot compare these latter works to those of Lu Xun with respect to whether they fall into the category of vital truth or spiritual-depth truth—the same way that we cannot compare Lu Xun's works to those of Dostoevsky with respect to whether they reach the level of spiritual-depth truth. When it comes to the dimension of vitality and spiritual depth, there remains a significant gap between the works of Shen Congwen,

Xiao Hong, and Eileen Chang, on one hand, and those of Lu Xun, on the other. Moreover, there are countless variations even among the former group of authors, just as there are between Chekhov, Turgenev, Tolstoy, and Dostoevsky.

However, in writing at the level of worldly truth, Shen Congwen and Eileen Chang offered us the possibility of transitioning from worldly truth to vital truth, and then on to spiritual-depth truth. Meanwhile, Lu Xun, Chekhov, Maupassant, Tolstoy, Turgenev, Dostoevsky, Balzac, Hugo, Flaubert, and Stendhal all showed us that even if you succeed in attaining vital or spiritual-depth truth, the literary works still won't be able to leave behind an examination of worldly matters. Sometimes, the more emphasis that is placed on vitality and spirit, the more one needs to attend to the world and worldly matters. This is truth's mutual reliance and indivisibility.

7 CAN THE PATH OF DEEP REALISM BE TRAVERSED?

Just as people must wear clothing and eat food, no national literature can ever escape the influence of realism. Realism is like sketching for modernist painting, and without a basis in sketching it is difficult to imagine the emergence of a modernist a painter like Picasso. It is impossible to conceive a national literature without realism, but it is also terrifying to imagine a situation in which every contemporary author is a realist.

In China, our literature must face two sets of backdrops. One is our current postsocialist era, which is something that cannot be changed yet must be confronted. The other is contemporary realism of today's world, which has crossed over from the twentieth to the twenty-first century. In historical terms the twenty-first century is a historical era, but in literary terms it is a strong and complex culture—and a literary background that we cannot ignore when writing fiction. What form will Chinese fiction take in the contemporary era? And what form *should* it take? Will realist fiction in the postsocialist period be able to continue exploring deeper and deeper? And where will it stop?

Speaking of realism's different levels of truth, we often complain that contemporary literature is not as good as modern literature or that contemporary authors cannot be compared to great modern authors like

Lu Xun or Shen Congwen. This kind of complaint uses realism or a traditional realistic perspective to evaluate literary achievement, despite the profound transformation that literature has undergone from the modern to the contemporary period. If we continue to rely on realism's different levels of truth to evaluate literature's merits, we will naturally discover that contemporary Chinese literature simply does not measure up to earlier literature from the modern period, just as contemporary authors cannot measure up to great modern authors like Lu Xun and Shen Congwen. This is because too many contemporary authors stop at the level of constructed truth or worldly truth, producing either works that are merely fatuous odes to revolutionary Chang'an or works that are perceived as stable and safe. When we discuss whether realist authors have managed to attain Lu Xun's level of vital truth, we ignore the social realities that contemporary authors must face, together with the authors' own cultural psychology. These are two significant barriers that impede realism's entry into deep truth.

Regardless of whether we are referring to literary production from the socialist period of the People's Republic of China (PRC), which is to say its first three decades, or from its postsocialist period, which is to say the following three decades, the common denominator in each case is socialism. But if you have socialism you will also have socialist realism, and naturally the core of socialist realism is what we have been calling constructed realism and constructed truth. The only difference is that during the PRC's first three decades, there was only constructed realism, and there couldn't be any other kind of literature; during the following three decades there continued to be constructed realism, but there emerged other kinds of literature and corresponding forms of truth. As a result, it currently isn't particularly difficult for realist fiction to transcend that kind of vacant truth, but what presents more of a problem is when the authors themselves are unwilling to do so.

This unwillingness to transcend vacant truth derives from the fact that the writing of constructed truth has become necessary for an author's survival. Most authors, if they lose this sort of writing, will lose everything. You could say that these authors are merely engaging in acts of flattery or a process of taking refuge, but when a certain kind of writing style becomes merely a form of living, and not a life itself, integrity is thereby reduced to a figurative coin of exchange. Transcending vacant truth becomes a challenge to basic integrity. Money and prestige may purchase an author's integrity, which in turn becomes a commodity in the socialist marketplace. The more that authors are willing to sell their integrity, the more capital and prestige they will be able to accumulate. It is said that no one needs to press the ox's head into the water to make it drink, since the ox will go to the river on its own accord. In reality, behind the "no one" in this expression there is actually what economists call an "invisible hand." This invisible hand holds a fistful of cash and prestige, and if authors see this, they will have no choice but to approach. In the past, this invisible hand would actively grab authors, but now it simply "recruits" them. Once constructed truth becomes an unspoken need that is shared by authors, readers, and power itself, it thereby becomes literature's "necessity." As a result, to ask these authors to put down their pens would be as unnecessary as asking them to violate the rule that no one needs to press an ox's head into the water to drink—not to mention the fact that contemporary literature now has a completely different composition and existence.

Apart from this invisible hand, another factor preventing contemporary authors' entry into a deeper truth is their inner heart—that is to say, the instinct and defense of the habits of their inner hearts. Literature cannot simply promote a resistance to and dissection of political ideology. In fact, this kind of resistance and dissection is the inverse of ideological writing; it is a new form of ideological writing. However, we must consider the social person (and not the individual) that is promoted by realism, because when separated from an analysis of society, this "person" cannot easily attain a height and depth that transcends society and politics. This is similar to the way Dostoevsky, when writing his spiritual-depth literature, did not—and, indeed, could not—escape the social contradictions that characterized nineteenth-century Russia. Meanwhile, for the several generations of Chinese authors who were writing under a regime of realism, the regime's attendant systems of censorship and self-censorship have reached the point where they circulate imperceptibly through the authors' veins. As a result, when we try to write, we find that this self-censoring mentality inevitably influences realist fiction's excavation of human nature and its exploration of living reality, whether we acknowledge it or not.

A third obstacle preventing contemporary authors' exploration of a deeper truth is the persuasiveness of canonical works written in the tradition of worldly-truth realism. Lu Xun himself consented to this, but now it has become dangerous. This unspoken but universally recognized danger allows authors and critics to perceive realism's broad horizon. With respect to tradition, this is an intimate inheritance; with respect to the future, this is a possible canonization; and with respect to power, readers, and critics, this is a general happiness in which everyone accepts one another. As a result, worldly realism becomes the site where the most intelligent, dedicated, and passionate authors can be found, but it is also the most significant barrier to realism's exploration of a deeper truth. It is precisely at this level that realism stops its exploration. Realist novels erect a dam to halt this advance, and the possibility of changing realism and demolishing this dam becomes a threshold that authors had previously surpassed but where now they merely stagnate.

This state of stagnation results from issues of construction and integrity, from the self-censoring psychology that develops under power, and from the canonization of worldly realism. In the end, these various factors all influence the possibility that an author might proceed from worldly truth to a deeper vital truth and spiritual-depth truth.

This is not a question of possibility but rather of ability.

To be more precise, it is not a question of ability but rather of will—of whether contemporary authors are willing to take this necessary step. This lack of will is the fundamental reason for the contemporary stagnation of realism's excavation toward deep reality.

2 Zero Causality

In order to write, I once went to a luxurious retreat far from the hubbub of the city, where the vegetation was as lush as though it were the earth's well-groomed hair. In autumn, as cold weather approached, the leaves fell, flowers wilted, and vegetation turned yellow. Peering through the bare tree branches, I noticed that a neighbor's wall was covered in inch-long ashy-black caterpillars that were all as thin as blades of straw and furry to the touch. When I looked more closely, however, I noticed that there weren't any caterpillars on the trees next to the wall, nor were there any hidden in the grass at the foot of the wall. When I went to a neighboring property on the other side of the forest, I found a similar scene: a multitude of ashy-black caterpillars covered the side of a white wall that was facing the sun, but there were none on any of the surrounding vegetation.

It turns out that these caterpillars can appear on forest walls, but only on the side warmed by the sun.

It turns out that these caterpillars were seeking warmth from sunlight.

It turns out that these caterpillars can reproduce not only on grass, trees, and riverbanks, but also on brick, cement, and steel walls. It is the same way if you take a lifeless rock and a dead piece of wood: as long as you give them a literary marriage license, they will be able to produce lawful children; over time, they will give birth to sandy dirt.

Franz Kafka's *The Metamorphosis* famously begins with a description of the protagonist transformed into an insect:

> As Gregor Samsa awoke one morning from uneasy dreams he found himself transformed in his bed into a gigantic insect. He was lying on his hard, as it were armor-plated, back and when he lifted his head a little he could see his domelike brown belly divided into stiff arched segments on top of which the bed quilt could hardly keep in position and was about to slide off completely. His numerous legs, which were pitifully thin compared to the rest of his bulk, waved helplessly before his eyes.[1]

When Kafka wrote these lines, he had no way of knowing they would help generate a vast transformation in twentieth-century literature, such that countless successors—including great authors—would gasp in astonishment. These opening lines beckon readers into the remarkable work, and regardless of whether we view the text as a short story or a novella, at the very least we can agree that it is a work of fiction.

As we read on, however, we encounter several questions, including questions relating to the author's power and position within the narrative.

Tolstoy recalls how when he was writing the part of *Anna Karenina* where the protagonist throws herself under the train, he slumped onto his desk and wept, because Anna's death made it impossible for him to control his emotions. He claims it was not he who wanted Anna to die, but rather it was her fate and personality that made it inevitable she would throw herself under the train. All great nineteenth-century realist authors have had the experience of not being in control of their characters' fate and instead finding themselves willing slaves to that same fate. In other words, for these authors, the greater the work, the more that the characters are able to determine their own fate. All great realist authors regard themselves as mere scribes or spokespeople and feel that their significance is superseded by that of their own fictional characters. It is as if, when Nora decided to leave home, Henrik Ibsen had no way of preventing her. An author is merely a narrator behind the scenes and has neither the power nor the ability to control a character's fate. The less control an author has over a character's fate, the more fresh, animated, natural, and lively the character will appear. Conversely, if an author is able to control a story's direction and a character's fate, the story and characters will appear rigid and feeble. In realism, accordingly, it is better when the author has less status and power, and when it comes to a character's fate, the best thing an author can do is to simply disappear.

Traditionally, great realist authors had to be slaves to their protagonists—this is the cardinal rule handed down to us by those immortal nineteenth-century works. It is only in second- and third-rank works that the author has the ability to control a character's fate, like a judge. However, the early twentieth-century emergence of Kafka, that emaciated and melancholy figure, changed all this. Rather than viewing an author as a mere slave and spokesperson for his fictional characters, Kafka instead elevated the author to the position of a personnel director or even a virtual emperor. This overturned the rule that the author should be subordinate to fictional characters, meaning that stories were no longer derived from a character's fate but rather were hatched directly from the author's mind.

"As Gregor Samsa awoke one morning from uneasy dreams he found himself transformed in his bed into a gigantic insect." This is a kind of hegemonic narration in which the author does not offer his characters or readers the slightest compromise or accommodation—just as an emperor can send his subjects to their death as though it were a gift, or the way a personnel director can revise or rewrite a case under his charge as he wishes. Kafka elevated the author's position and power, and when he arranged for Gregor Samsa to be transformed into an insect, Samsa thereby became an insect—and if he had wanted Samsa to become a pig or a dog, Samsa would have become a pig or a dog. The narrator no longer attempts to accommodate the reader's reading habits or sense of realism, nor does he pay any heed to whether a character's fate accords with what life experience would suggest is possible.

When I discovered that the wall near my retreat could spawn insects, I realized that the underlying conditions for this phenomenon are autumn coolness and that the wall must be facing the sun and surrounded by vegetation. If it isn't autumn, and if there isn't lush foliage nearby, a wall won't produce insects—the same way that bricks and stones cannot begin to copulate and reproduce on their own. However, Kafka didn't care about any of this, and instead he simply wanted Gregor Samsa to change into an insect overnight. If one must specify the conditions for Samsa's transformation, it would simply be that the previous night he had "uneasy dreams." As for what precisely Samsa dreamed about and what were his reactions, Kafka couldn't be troubled to give his readers any explanation. This made people wonder whether the real meaning of the opening *The Metamorphosis* might be that Samsa's uneasy dreams might be something that Kafka had unintentionally written about, and not something he had deliberately planned. Or perhaps they were something that Kafka—given his imperial authorial powers—could casually fire off and then leave everyone hanging in suspense. In sum, enabling conditions were no longer important, and if the author wanted a character to become an insect, the character would become an insect.

The author has precisely this kind of power and position, and can decide everything. It used to be said that "literary arts are human arts," and "the pen should follow the character,"[2] but in *The Metamorphosis* these writing practices derived from nineteenth-century experience and achievements became as worthless as a human appendix. The imperial seal Kafka bequeathed unto twentieth-century authors represented a power that doesn't necessarily need to be used. You don't have to show off your position in your writing, but this doesn't mean that you don't have the power that is associated with that position. Kafka's *The Metamorphosis*, *The Castle*, and *The Trial* granted twentieth-century authors a proof and authorization for a different writing path—thereby offering a precedent and a possibility for his successors' later claims to a "hegemonic narrative" and "imperial position." This would also grant rationality a legitimate position within the regime of the sensible. The result was that the "artificiality" that novels had once possessed was no longer perceived as being a flaw and object of ridicule. When we combine this artificiality with the unlimited power that the author claims during the writing process, the artificiality is no longer perceived as a flaw but rather has the potential to become a new individuality.

The remaining question is: When Kafka liberated authors from their enslavement to their own fictional characters and granted them the possibility of attaining a hegemonic, imperial narration, did that mean that we, as readers, were released from our enslavement to the story's fictional characters only to became slaves to Kafka's narrative? Did we thereby become slaves to absurdity and alienation? This is Gregor Samsa's question, which we must face as we approach the narration.

Twentieth-century literature is both the beneficiary and the victim of Gregor Samsa's question, and this is also the liberation and the new constraints that we currently face as writers.

2 GREGOR SAMSA'S SECOND QUESTION: A STORY'S BIDIRECTIONAL LINE OF CAUSALITY

Following Gregor Samsa's transformation into an insect, the novella's narrative has two dimensions: the implicit story of Samsa himself, which is presented with minimal assistance, and the story of the external changes that Samsa's transformation produces in his family, his workplace, and so forth. We might call the former the hidden or secondary story, and the latter the visible or main story.

The hidden or secondary story of Samsa becoming an insect acts like an announcer who welcomes the main story onto the stage, and after offering a preparatory speech the announcer then either steps off stage or stands discretely in a corner, occasionally offering an explanation as the main story proceeds. In this way, the main story shapes the development of the secondary story.

The Metamorphosis consists of three parts. The first focuses on Samsa's confusion and anxiety after becoming an insect, while the second and third focus on the confusion and anxiety that Samsa's transformation inspires in others. In the hidden story, Kafka devotes the least amount of attention to the description of Samsa's actual transformation, and in the thirty-thousand-character novella (in translation), this transformation is addressed in only six or seven passages, each of which consists of only a few sentences of simple explanation. Added together, these passages amount to only about one-thirtieth of the entire work.

For instance, Kafka's first relatively detailed description of the insect that Samsa becomes appears near the beginning of the work:

He felt a slight itching up on his belly; slowly pushed himself on his back nearer to the top of the bed so that he could lift his head more easily; identified the itching place which was surrounded by many small white spots the nature of which he could not understand and made to touch it with a leg, but drew the leg back immediately, for the contact made a cold shiver run through him.[3]

Later there are descriptions of how "he was so uncommonly broad. He would have needed arms and hands to hoist himself up; instead he had only the numerous little legs which never stopped waving in all directions and which he could not control in the least," and "at first he slipped down a few times from the polished surface of the chest, but at length with a last heave he stood upright; he paid no more attention to the pains in the lower part of his body, however they smarted. Then he let himself fall against the back of a nearby chair, and clung with his little legs to the edges of it."[4]

Eventually, the narrative describes how

the rotting apple in his back and the inflamed area around it, all covered with soft dust, already hardly troubled him.... Since she happened to have the long-handled broom in her hand she tried to tickle him up with it from the doorway. When that too produced no reaction she felt provoked and poked at him a little harder, and only when she had pushed him along the floor without meeting any resistance was her attention aroused. It did not take her long to establish the truth of the matter, and her eyes widened, she let out a whistle, yet did not waste much time over it but tore open the door of the Samsas' bedroom and yelled into the darkness at the top of her voice: "Just look at this, it's dead; it's lying here dead and done for!"[5]

There isn't an excessive amount of attention devoted to these accounts beginning with Samsa's initial transformation and concluding with his death, nor is the reader's imagination piqued by detailed descriptions of the insect's living situation or its life circumstances. In fact, it could even be said that following Samsa's transformation, Kafka does not use his imperial position as an author to describe the daily life and life processes of the insect itself, and instead devotes all his attention to the internal changes that Samsa-as-insect undergoes, together with the external changes that Samsa inspires in his external surroundings, in other people, and in the outside world.

This, in turn, raises the following issues:

1   Samsa's transformation into an insect is not the story's primary objective, but rather it is the reason for the story's development. It is secondary to the work's main story.

2   The development and changes undergone by the main story rely on the unfolding and advancement of the secondary story. Without the secondary story, there would be no main story, the same way that without a cause there can be no result.

For instance, the reason the brick-and-cement wall mentioned in this chapter became covered in grey caterpillars was because the wall was located in an insect-infested forest. The wall's location in the forest was the cause, and regardless of where precisely the insects were born, with the arrival of autumn they must seek a warm location facing the sun. Without these enabling conditions, the wall would never have become covered in caterpillars. In short, all results are determined by an initial cause and a continuous sequence of succeeding causes.

This is precisely how *The Metamorphosis* begins. Because Gregor Samsa became an insect, he was initially unable to get out of bed. Later, every time he took a step, he would leave behind an abundance of mucus. This process continued until ultimately the apple thrown by Samsa's father "landed right on his back and sank in."[6]

After Samsa became an insect, his father transitioned from surprise to disgust, until finally the insect became a corpse, thereby giving readers a chilling sense of relief. Samsa's younger sister transitioned from initial surprise to attentive care, to eventual alienation. His boss transitioned from initial terror to eventual flight. There were also the tenants living in Samsa's house, who went from first seeing Samsa's transformation to eventually leaving the house altogether. After insect-Samsa died at the end of the story, his beloved mother, father, and sister "left the apartment together, which was more than they had done for months, and went by tram into the open country outside the town. The tram, in which they were the only passengers, was filled with warm sunshine. Leaning comfortably back in their seats they canvassed their prospects for the future, and it appeared on closer inspection that these were not at all bad."[7] When the story reaches this point, the warmth felt by Samsa's family leaves us utterly cold, and the reason for all this lies in how "as Gregor Samsa awoke one morning from uneasy dreams he found himself transformed in his bed into a gigantic insect."

All the world's stories unfold within a matrix not only of space and time, but also of cause and effect. For some authors (such as Marcel Proust), time and space are particularly important, while for others (a group that also includes Proust), cause and effect are even more crucial. Time and space are the story's natural existence, and as long as a story is born, time and space will necessarily accompany it. However, even if time and space are continuously positioned in front of an author's eyes and in the author's hands, to be accessed as easily as taking something from one's pocket, the cause that permits a story to be established and develop cannot always be at the author's beck and call. In a good novel, causality is a battlefield—and the battle is not only between cause and effect, but also between causality and the author him- or herself. Because cause and effect are so critical for a story, they inevitably surpass all a novel's other elements. Cause determines effect, even as the effect frequently changes the original cause. This is how wars begin, and how stories develop.

A causal relationship is not only a story's skeleton but also the marrow that nourishes the story's bones as well as the soul of the story, plot, and characters. When an author is conceiving a story, he or she is frequently constrained by causality. Without causality there can be no story, but causality is like the chains that constrain the story's wanton development. It is every author's secret desire to be liberated from these constraints, the same way that outlaws feel resentment toward the law. A perfect match of cause and effect is a law of storytelling to which readers, critics, and authors have unconsciously agreed. All an author's efforts with respect to a story and its fictional characters are directed toward attempting to break free from the constraints of existing causality and create a new kind of causal relationship—just as an outlaw wants to create his or her own rules. In this respect Kafka's novella conforms to the storytelling provisions that have been in place for millennia, while simultaneously breaking from these same provisions and establishing an entirely new causality. Both the secondary story that ensues after Samsa's transformation into an insect and the main story that is thereby set in motion are committed to provisions governing the work's causality. However, if we consider only the point—the shocking point—of Samsa's overnight transformation into an insect, this is like a spark that ignited the causal rules that have governed storytelling for millennia and which, in the process, provided the twentieth century's "new stories" with a new causal foundation and space, thereby allowing subsequent authors to shatter the old causal constraints and providing them with new opening through which they might breathe or even break free.

3 GREGOR SAMSA'S THIRD QUESTION: ZERO CAUSALITY

Stories are born out of an author's reinterpretation of—and resistance to—causality and are a result of the author's assiduous attempts to create a new causal order. However, there are two categories of authors when it comes to attempting to create a new causal order. One struggles to break through existing causal rules and causal orders, while the other simply jumps beyond the three realms to start over again and establish an entirely new causal relationship, creating and confirming new rules:

> Kafka falls into the latter category. Indeed, he is the category's founder and pioneer.
> Kafka provided us with "zero causality."
> Zero causality is causeless effect.

The Metamorphosis is the best realization of this sort of causeless effect. The work has become a twentieth-century classic thanks to its pioneering role in establishing this new causality, or what I am calling zero causality.

Gregor Samsa became an insect overnight. But why did he become an insect? Who made him become an insect? How did he become an insect? What are the physical and physiological conditions that would permit a human to become an insect? What was the process by which he became an insect? For Kafka, none of these questions had any importance. "As Gregor Samsa awoke one morning from uneasy dreams he found himself transformed in his bed into a gigantic insect." This becomes a fixed reality, and having uneasy dreams is not so much the condition Kafka gives for Samsa's transformation into an insect but rather simply his way of teasing his readers. There is no discussion or recollection of the process by which Samsa became an insect, and neither are there any supplemental explanations or allusions to the process within the story itself. The new causality has already begun, and the author cannot look back to the original cause; the enormous gap left behind by that absent cause is a black hole that befuddles readers and critics alike. This incomparably deep and empty black hole is also the eye of zero causality staring back at us. It regards us with skepticism, and regardless of how we might attempt to raise questions, it always answers with silence. When we anxiously seek answers from the story, Kafka does not offer any explanation for why Samsa became an insect and instead simply uses rational and methodical narrative to tell us the story of what happens after Samsa's transformation. Meanwhile, even after the insect is found dead, "it struck both Mr. and Mrs. Samsa, almost at the same moment, as they became aware of their daughter's increasing vivacity, that in spite of all the sorrow of recent times, which had made her cheeks pale, she had bloomed into a pretty girl with a good figure. They grew quieter and half unconsciously exchanged glances of complete agreement, having come to the conclusion that it would soon be time to find a good husband for her. And it was like a confirmation of their new dreams and excellent intentions that at the end of their journey their daughter sprang to her feet first and stretched her young body."[8] This is the novella's warm, soothing ending, and it is also Kafka's final answer to our questions about a "causeless cause."

This is how the causeless cause abruptly appears, which leaves readers feeling completely helpless. A plot unfolds with this causeless cause as its premise, and the result is formed in the same way. For instance, whether you believe it or not, there may be an apple growing not on a tree but rather in thin air. Meanwhile, what is most convincing about *The Metamorphosis* is not the author's refusal to discuss this kind of zero causality but rather this causality's seamless arrival. There is no reason for Samsa's transformation into an insect (or, at least, we are not told the reason), but because he became an insect, an unusual yet at the same time thoroughly mundane and realistic story unfolds. This story includes the parents' initial surprise and subsequent revulsion at their son's transformation; the sister's initial shock, her subsequent attentive care, and her eventual alienation; together with the outside world's isolation and eventual rejection of Samsa following his transformation.

Each of these elements generally conforms to everyday reality. The story is premised on a cause that arrives out of nowhere, but it offers an effect that appears completely realistic, with no extraneous details. It is this combination that produces zero causality's combination of balance and mystery—like a scale with text on one side and empty air on the other, and regardless of how much text is placed on the first side, as long as it consists merely of mundane plots and details, the scale will remain balanced.

Among Kafka's short stories (which, though relatively few in number, are nevertheless extremely rich), there is "Blumfeld, an Elderly Bachelor," whose protagonist is lonely and "only wants a companion," whereupon a pair of bouncing white celluloid balls suddenly appear in his home. Blumfeld finds these balls very novel and comes to feel that he has acquired a new companion. In the end, however, he discovers that he can't stand the sound of the balls and therefore gives them to a neighbor's child, after which he returns to the lonely tranquility of his former life.[9] There is also "The Bucket Rider," whose protagonist rides a coal bucket through the air to seek aid from his coal dealer. On his bucket, the protagonist proceeds "at a regular canter; often I am upraised as high as the first story of a house; never do I sink as low as the house doors."[10] In "The Hunger Artist," the protagonist fasts for more than forty days straight, and in the process he transforms his hunger into a kind of high art.[11] "The Burrow" describes the restlessness and anxiety that an animal feels living in its "house," while in "The Judgment," the son, in accordance with the judgment issued by his father, proceeds, "like the distinguished gymnast he had once been in his youth," to leap to his death from a bridge.[12] Regardless of whether we view these works as examples of absurdity, exaggeration, irony, or humor, they all deploy an unyielding and hegemonic narration extrapolated from the traditional causality that one finds in realist fiction, thereby letting the causeless effect of zero causality enter and permeate the story and its fictional characters.

With these stories, Kafka collided with and broke through the traditional causal logic and rationality that had been collectively established by readers, authors, and critics, thereby granting fiction a new narrative order—absurdity. This, in turn, positioned Kafka as the virtual father of twentieth-century modernism. Ultimately, however, it was

The Metamorphosis that truly changed the narrative order, establishing a new zero-causal narrative. It was the novel's perfect union of entirely mundane examples of causeless cause and causeless effect, on the one hand, and everyday life experience, on the other, that put the scale of zero-causal narrative order into perfect balance. By contrast, because of zero causality's incompleteness and the alienated nature of the link to everyday experience in works such as "The Bucket Rider," "Blumfeld, the Elderly Bachelor," and "The Hunger Artist," in the end these short stories failed to reach the exquisite perfection of the narrative order we find in *The Metamorphosis*.

With the establishment of a new narrative order grounded in zero causality, the author's reliance on a shared experience with readers becomes particularly important, regardless of what kind of linguistic or cultural background the author might have. When the story's plotline departs from everyday life experience, the new narrative order becomes fortuitous, legendary, and even comical. Kafka's works are replete with an authority and an attitude toward writing that make readers anguished and respectful. Fellow authors inevitably feel compelled to bow down at Kafka's feet whenever they read his observation that:

> On the handle of Balzac's walking-stick: I break all obstacles.
> On mine: All obstacles break me.
> The common factor is "all."[13]

In a story like "The Bucket Rider," we observe Kafka's enormous sympathy for his protagonist, but because of zero causality, he cannot avoid bringing in a kind of absurdity, which makes readers nostalgic for the sort of power and narrative causality found in a work like *Little Match Girl*. Fortunately, *The Metamorphosis* firmly established a new zero-causal narrative order, while in works like "The Bucket Rider" and "Blumfeld, the Elderly Bachelor," causality and narrative structure come to acquire a new significance.

We are grateful for the new narrative order and the perfect synthesis of that new order with mundane life experience that *The Metamorphosis* established. All of Kafka's works are similarly indebted to the meaning of life in the new order that the zero-causal narrative order of *The Metamorphosis* granted them.

Most of Kafka's works are unfinished. All three of his novels are unfinished, and of his short stories, at most six or seven are complete. This may be a result of the fact that Kafka liked to begin writing before he had finished plotting out a work, and consequently even as the work was approaching completion, he still did not know how to give it a final punctuation mark. Alternatively, it may be because of the way in which this sort of zero causality destabilized the narrative, the story therefore lacked sufficient conditions, and he didn't know in which direction to take it—meaning that he often put the story's conclusion on hold, like a ship that is abandoned by its crew before it reaches shore. Among realist authors, there are very few who are able to stop writing a story before reaching the conclusion—unless they are impeded by health issues or other external factors. Kafka, however, was different. As for why so many of his works are unfinished, apart from the fact that most of his surviving works are from manuscripts that he had asked his friend Max Brod to burn after his death, the more important factor is probably that Kafka truly did not know how to complete a story.

This situation would appear to be not unrelated to zero causality.

Zero causality is like wandering through a wasteland, and without roads or road signs you would have no way of knowing where you are headed or where you should stop. Alternatively, it could be compared to an author who is unwilling to use different seasons as a causal condition, and who wants to have an apple ripen despite not knowing under what circumstances apples would ordinarily turn red and start producing a delicious fragrance. But precisely for this reason, it is ultimately irrelevant whether K—the protagonist of Kafka's unfinished masterpiece *The Castle*—ultimately settled down in the village at the foot of the castle. The work's conclusion doesn't matter to readers in the same way that it would have if Anna Karenina had selected an alternate way of killing herself. Readers of *The Castle* focus on whether K will be able to enter the castle, but what does the castle symbolize? What is its true meaning?

"There was nothing to be seen of Castle Mount, for mist and darkness surrounded it, and not the faintest glimmer of light showed where the great castle lay. K stood on the wooden bridge leading from the road to the village for a long time, looking up at what seemed to be a void."[14] Throughout the work, this "void" lingers in the reader's mind, and the more difficult that it becomes for K to enter the castle, and the more he persists in his efforts, the more mysterious the mist-shrouded castle becomes and the more heavily the castle becomes lodged in readers' chests. Even at the end of the work, readers still cannot determine why precisely K is unable to enter the castle—this the black hole of the novel's meaning. Within this black hole some see bureaucratic corruption, others see the meaninglessness of institutionalized society, others see an allusion to the consumption of human life, and others see simply an absurd paradox. These are all different explanations of the black hole manifested by zero causality. It is as though everyone were peering into a bottomless well, and using the light from the opening of the well to discern different scenes and reflections in the dark murkiness of the well's interior.

Indeed, once zero causality is perfectly combined with the real world and with people's mundane experiences, it will necessarily manifest fiction's black hole of meaning.

We often say that Gregor Samsa became an insect due to social alienation and industrial society's suppression of the individual. This kind of understanding grants *The Metamorphosis* a broad and deep significance, but I wonder whether Kafka would have been somewhat startled if he were able to be reborn and could hear this sort of interpretation. On the other hand, it is also possible that Kafka might not have been surprised at all by this response, and perhaps he might even have been rather pleased. In the end, the author's zero causality granted his novel a black hole of meaning, and he doesn't have the power to prevent readers from forming their own thoughts, judgments, and conjectures. Why is it that on the scale of zero causality, the novella's narrative is able to maintain a balance with its reading? It is because on one side of the scale there is the real world, while on the other side there is the weight of the black hole. The larger, more complex, and breathtaking the reality on one side, the more weighty and more significant the invisible black hole on the other side.

We know that the real factor preventing K from entering the castle is not the village and the villagers, nor is it the castle's authority and institutions, but rather it is Kafka himself and his zero-causal writing practice. It is as if Kafka were saying, "There is no reason, or at least no easily explained reason, why I made it impossible for K—and also for you, my readers—to enter the castle." This is the causeless cause that drives the entire novel, and it is the foundation for the work's entire creation and development. As for K's difficulty in securing a housing permit upon arriving in the village, the trouble he brings the innkeeper, the difficulty he encounters when he meets the village mayor, the affection he feels for Frieda, and his visit to the school where he is offered a temporary post—in all of these various plotlines we observe the objectively real K, and the entanglements and struggles he encounters trying to reach the castle that he must visit in order to settle down in the village. Here, a strong causeless cause constrains and drives the story's direction and the characters' fate.

Traditional realism makes characters greater than authors, while modernist literature places authors above characters.

In the nineteenth century, authors often achieved fame because of the vitality of their fictional characters. In the twentieth century, by contrast, fictional characters are often discussed based on the vitality of the authors who created them. This reversal originated with Kafka and his zero causality. Because on one side of the zero-causal story balance there is reality and on the other side there is an invisible black hole of meaning, in our reading process we therefore feel that the external world's stories, characters, events, and behaviors become agglomerated with this anti-realist black hole of meaning. This black hole determines the story's reality effect, and the resulting representation of reality also encourages readers' speculation about the black hole. As for the significance of *The Castle*, once could say that "the work's central theme involves the unbearable anguish that people experience while trying to enter Heaven, while others believe that the work expresses the author's own feelings of anxiety and loneliness. Others, meanwhile, believe that the work fully and vividly reflects the uncrossable gulf that exists between Austria-Hungary's bureaucracy and its common people."[15] In other words, *The Castle* is trying to tell us that "the truth people pursue, regardless whether it be freedom, security, or the law, they all exist. However, this absurd world offers people all sorts of obstacles, and regardless of how hard you try, you'll never be able to reach your goals, such that in the end you must conclude with defeat."[16] These interpretations, which feature a combination of foreign and Chinese cultural elements, are all correct, but they are also all incorrect. Because of the existence of the story's black hole of meaning, every reader has the right to their own perspective and interpretation, but at the same time each reader is necessarily limited by his or her own reading experience.

This is similar to how everyone simultaneously understands and yet doesn't understand the Qing dynasty classic *Dream of the Red Chamber*.

It is said that "when humans think, God laughs." However, if humans *don't* think, will God instead laugh to the point of tears? The issue lies not in seeing something in zero causality's black hole of meaning but rather in whether an author, in the course of writing, is able offer readers one or more black holes of meaning. For instance, a man and woman meet in another couple's apartment, but it is only after a long discussion that they finally realize they both arrived on the same train, they both came from the same location, and furthermore they both live on the same street, in the same building, and in the same apartment. They discover that they sleep in the same bed, eat the same food, and even share a child they conceived as husband and wife. Why is this couple so alienated from one another? What are the circumstances by which they can be husband and wife, yet not even recognize one another? There is no "because," only a "therefore." There is only black hole of meaning that was set up in advance by zero causality. Were it not for this black hole of meaning, then for readers and critics zero causality would lose its reason for being, and within the fictional work it would in turn lose its need to exist.

3 Full Causality

When in 1912 Kafka composed his landmark novella that exemplified zero causality, he compelled us to look back at the preceding period—and particularly a development process that had unfolded over the preceding century or two, and which ultimately culminated in a pinnacle of realism that contemporary authors and readers continue to love and cherish. Many writing rules specify that the original method of displaying a story and the causal relationship between a character's words and actions involves a rigorously mature "full causality." Sometimes this type of full causality seeps in from outside, and other times it spurts out from inside; to develop full characters, deep thought, and an extended story, sometimes it uses a readily perceptible causality to drive the plot and characters, and other times it uses a hidden causality that readers can only sense but are unable to touch.

It is difficult to find any works by canonical realist authors that feature effect without a cause, or result without condition. A fundamental rule to which all realist authors adhere is that virtually all plots and characters must exist for a reason. This is a strict requirement that was collectively established by authors and readers, and those who violated it were viewed as deviants and offenders. Although life and laws could not discipline these offenders, readers, commentators, and literary historians could punish their transgressions with indifference and mockery. This was William Shakespeare's experience, as well as

Kafka's. Dostoevsky worked diligently and created great works, but he was not as warmly received as some of his contemporaries who wrote more conventional realistic works—this was also because he deviated from a regime of full causality. In the end, however, time heals all, and smiles upon those authors who use a violation of full causality to acquire a unique and excellent artistic value.

The most notable characteristic of so-called full-causal writing is the completeness and equivalence of its causality. By completeness I mean causality's ubiquitous presence within a story, whereby if a leaf falls from a tree and it isn't autumn, then you must explain to readers why the leaf has fallen. Without causality, a story cannot develop and characters cannot act—this is causality's life-determining essence. By equivalence, I mean that under full causality, the scale of the cause must be equivalent to that of the result. If there is a certain kind of condition, there has to be a similar kind of conclusion, resulting in a complete equivalence of cause and effect. For instance, if you have a fruit tree and from one year to the next the weather conditions are the same and you put the same amount of effort into cultivating it, the tree will necessarily yield the same amount of fruit. However, if you have the same weather and put in the same amount of effort, yet your returns are either significantly greater or significantly less than they had been the previous year, or perhaps this time you have no returns at all, you will certainly feel dispirited and frustrated. On the surface this latter result might appear inexplicable, but if you look more carefully you will inevitably discover that some variable has in fact changed. These changes that you didn't initially notice will turn out to have altered the underlying conditions— for instance, whether it was a big year for fruit cultivation or for insect pests. If you take into account factors that you may have previously overlooked, the relationship between cause and effect will indeed turn out to be fully balanced, necessary, and consistent.

Accordingly, when writing under a regime of full causality, what authors need to describe are not the sorts of obvious causes that readers can easily observe in their everyday lives—which is to say, visible causes. Instead, authors need to attend to the sorts of invisible causes that readers might not notice were it not for these literary works, or causes that might be visible but otherwise appear to be incommensurate. Through these works readers can discover causal relations they had previously suspected might exist, and this kind of reassessment is precisely the kind of response that authors seek. When autumn arrives, trees must always shed their leaves, and a hundred pounds of cause must always yield a hundred pounds of effect—this is simply common sense, and it isn't literature. By contrast, if spring arrives and leaves don't turn green, or if a hundred pounds of cause yields a thousand or even ten thousand pounds of effect, or perhaps it doesn't yield any effect at all—now *that* is literature. However, when an author wants to transform the latter types of causality into literature, it is necessary to methodically develop the work's plot, subplots, and characters to uncover why vegetation doesn't turn green with the arrival of spring, or why a hundred pounds of cause might yield a thousand pounds of effect—to uncover this hidden nine thousand nine hundred pounds of cause. Conversely, when ten thousand pounds of cause yields only one hundred pounds of effect, then it is incumbent upon authors, in their writing, to uncover the remaining nine thousand nine hundred pounds of effect that was obscured or hidden, destroyed or lost. In the end, however, authors still need to demonstrate to their readers the ubiquitous completeness of full causality, together with the full consistency of the relationship between cause and effect and between condition and result.

The reason people love literature is because the causality in those works is complete and necessary. This is full causality. However, what people actually experience in real life is always doubt and hesitation, or even outright disparity and opposition. What a story needs to focus on are those causal relations that should exist but have not yet appeared, or situations where there seems to be a stark disparity or direct opposition between cause and effect. Under an author's realist pen, these hidden, disparate, or mutually opposed elements are slowly revealed until the reader can finally observe those lost, reversed, or destroyed causal relations that exist below those hidden or incommensurate surface realities—*this* is why realist literature moves people. Every work an author writes is for the purpose of demonstrating the full equivalence of cause and effect. People, events, things, and spaces all develop within a realm of full causality. There are no people or events that are not causally entangled. One of the key conditions of realist writing is that it must develop these various obscured, hidden, or transformed causal relations. In the end, the process of creating characters and transmitting thought under these causal conditions will reveal the existence of those causal relations that readers cannot see, as well as the completeness of this causal logic.

In Tolstoy's *Resurrection*, when Nekhludoff sees Maslova in the courtroom, why does he immediately begin to confess? It is because he felt continually tortured by the struggles between his inner "angel" and his inner "animal." In the end, the reason Maslova didn't marry her beloved Nekhludoff and instead married the political prisoner Simonson is not because she loved Simonson more but rather because, in her eyes, he was "so wonderful (as she expressed it) as those [political prisoners] whom she was now going with she had not only never met but could not even have imagined."[1] By contrast, Nekhludoff was able to betray his noble background precisely because he came to realize the darkness of the tsarist system and the cruelty and hypocrisy of the nobility. All vicissitudes have their underlying causes, even if they involve merely a character's accidental glimpse or slight change of heart. *Resurrection* offers nothing but a diagram of complete, ubiquitous full causality wherein Maslova's bright spirit and Nekhludoff's eventual spiritual transformation from darkness to light all have their own rationality and necessity based on a combination of the characters' worldly, circumstantial, and inner experiences. The more complicated the cause, the more admirable and unforgettable the result; and the more a result is found to be unforgettable, the more the corresponding conditions must be perceived as necessary.

Great works are continually searching within this kind of obscured causality, and once an author discovers the proposed cause, this will determine the story's conclusion and the emotional response that the characters will elicit in readers. The more hidden and unknowable the relationship between cause and effect is in an author's development of causal relations, the greater your value will be. However, the method of proposing and developing this causal relationship will be dependent on the author's personality and skill. Together, these factors will not only yield a causal writing, they will determine the work's ultimate success or failure. In contrast to a work like Alexandre Dumas's *The Count of Montecristo*, which displays primarily the causal relationships undergone by events, *Resurrection* instead focuses on the causal relations that exist in people's souls. The former reveals the hidden causality of events in a step-by-step process, while the latter takes causal relations that no one recognizes and then cultivates them within his imagination. The former can be called visible causality, while the latter can be called hidden, deep, or psychological causality.

In full-causal writing, the pursuit of hidden or deep causality is the ideal of every realist author.

We may be unable to determine which of Tolstoy's masterworks—*War and Peace, Anna Karenina*, and *Resurrection*—is the greatest. In full-causal narration, however, the unfolding and revelation of causal relations hidden in the depths of society and characters' souls is progressive and transformative, and when it comes to the causal relations hidden in the souls of his fictional characters, Dostoevsky succeeded in going much further and deeper than Tolstoy—to the point that a light from the depths of the characters' souls was able to illuminate his readers and the works of later authors. From the nineteenth century's full-causal writings, cause and result are mutually entangled and influence one another. Cause and effect often become merged, and not only does cause determine effect, effect also creates cause and can even transform the original cause into a new one. This is an interlocking story, in which abundant and complex characters and full-causal realism are expanded to become a power that people can accept. However, from the perspective of whether stories can be read, virtually all authors from this period—including figures such as Balzac, Hugo, Flaubert, and Charles Dickens—pursued not only seamless, believable, and fully causal stories and characters but also the causal relations between characters and society. Regardless of whether it is because of society that you are able to reveal people's interior visible causality, or it is because of characters' souls that you are able to reveal society's and the world's hidden causality; and regardless of whether it was because of sunlight shining directly down on the former causal relationships, or because of a gradual warming of the revelatory writing of hidden-cause stories—these are all means by which nineteenth-century realism advanced. However, there is one point that helped spawn twentieth-century literature and its hybrid of zero causality and partial causality: this was hidden causality's power and force, and not the visible causality that is located in full causality.

2 THE LIMITS OF FULL CAUSALITY

After full-causal realist fiction reached its pinnacle in the nineteenth century, authors and readers began to perceive its inherent limits—the same way that although it may indeed be beautiful when vegetation turns green every spring, if it were *always* spring people would inevitably come to feel bored and constrained. Characters in full-causal novels are social beings, and their personal experience reflects on the status of the collective. A rule on which Chinese critics and readers often secretly agree is that a work should aspire to being "superior to life," and not only does this concisely sum up the full-causal collective experience, it also captures the birth and development of the "social individual" in the tradition of nineteenth-century literature. In Lu Xun's famous novella, for instance, Ah Q's head is in one location, his torso is in another, and his arms and legs are somewhere else altogether—this is a canonical rule for creating canonical fictional characters, and the necessary path for the birth of social individuals.

Realism's fondness for collective experience is like the general, vague, yet sincere affection that a farmer feels for his land, and while a farmer loves everything on the land, each autumn he doesn't harvest everything but instead carefully selects what he wants. Moreover, the crops he selects are not necessarily what he himself likes but rather what he thinks others will want. Similarly, realist novels belong to readers, while the act of writing them belongs to authors. Full causality, meanwhile, is a consensus shared by readers and authors. One story after another proves the completeness and equivalence of causal relations that readers have not personally observed or experienced. In realist writing, one kind of author may search for this sort of causal completeness and equivalence in social and secular relations while another may look for confirmation in the depths of a character's soul. Both, however, understand the following two points:

1 The more collective the experience on which you rely in your writing, the more resonant your works will be.
2 The more your works enter hidden causality (using people's souls, and not social and secular reality, to demonstrate the correctness of full causality), the more likely it is that your works will become canonized.

Efforts on both these fronts, however, inevitably commit the same error, which is that they overvalue collective experience and undervalue individual experience. Just as Dostoevsky was able to write about the true reality of the depths of people's souls, the soul he was able to offer his readers was ultimately unable to extricate itself from the shrouds of collectivism. The reason everyone who reads about Raskolnikov's trembling soul can feel their own soul trembling is because his soul actually belongs to everyone—it is a soul that all readers share. In realist writing that relies on collective experience, does this most unique and unusual individual experience have any significance? And do people's dreamscapes and fleeting consciousness—these most individual of things—ultimately have any significance? Among Kafka's major works, there is not even one that does not represent a synthesis of his distinctive individual experience, emotions, sensitivity, and imagination. Just imagine what Kafka's writings would have looked like if they had appeared not in twentieth-century literature's emphasis on individual experience but rather in the context of nineteenth-century realism's emphasis on collective experience. Among the nineteenth century's great authors, it is difficult to find anyone with a background comparable to Kafka's. This is not to say that there did not exist authors with distinctive individual experiences but rather that the distinctive individual was covered, ignored, and killed by the strength of the collective experience. It was not until the appearance of Kafka—or the moment his works were finally recognized—that modernist writing finally began to gradually liberate individual experience.

Another disadvantage of full-causal writing lies in the way it suppresses the contingencies of ordinary life. Full causality insists that every effect must have a corresponding cause, and every result must have a corresponding condition. Everything has a necessary origin and destination. The words, actions, and fates of characters such as Anna Karenina, Katyusha Maslova, Rodion Raskolnikov, Eugénie Grandet, Father Goriot, and Emma Rouault are all fully determined and are not influenced by contingency. Even if there were an element of chance, that contingency would still be embedded within a larger regime of necessity. Within this sort of full-causal regime in which everything is strictly determined, however, it would be impossible for Joseph K, in Kafka's *The Trial*, to wake up one morning and find himself in such a bizarre predicament despite not having done anything wrong. In full-causal literature, it is completely senseless for someone walking under an empty sky to be killed when a rock appears out of the blue and hits them on the head. In the real world, however, people are embedded within a regime not of causality but rather of chance, just as Joseph K's fate was determined not by necessity but rather by contingency.

Another key difference between zero-causal and full-causal writing—and one of the most significant limitations of full-causal writing—involves literature's approach to contingency's legitimacy and rationality, together with contingency's own demands for, and control over, necessity within a story. While it would be senseless, in full-causal writing, for someone walking down the road to get killed by a rock that appears out of nowhere, within a zero-causal work this sort of development could have a more innovative, complex, and deeper significance. By revealing the existence of contingency and granting it human and literary value, what zero causality seeks to implement is precisely what full causality either cannot perceive or else deliberately conceals. Based on these two sets of limitations, the twentieth century offered a new beginning. In particular, after zero causality became more widespread and began to receive a surprising amount of recognition, there emerged a long procession of philosophers, poets, playwrights, and novelists who all worshipped Kafka's work. Renowned novelists like Albert Camus, Jorge Luis Borges, Italo Calvino, Philip Roth, Vladimir Nabokov, and Gabriel García Márquez used their writings to express their understanding of Kafka's texts (as opposed to his life and environment), together with their own struggle with and supplementation of the limitations of full causality. In these authors' works, their emphasis on individual experience and on the contingencies of people within a collective experience makes the stories' causality undergo a subtle, peculiar, and novel transformation, thereby allowing a new causal regime to emerge.

In this way there appeared a new form of fiction with a completely different aesthetic effect and, like zero causality, it subsequently enjoyed incalculable success.

4 Partial Causality

1 PARTIAL CAUSALITY

When Gabriel García Márquez was writing *One Hundred Years of Solitude*, he never expected that he would go on to become a global celebrity. Instead, he assumed that if his local publishing house could manage to sell at least five thousand copies of the novel, that would be very respectable. He certainly didn't anticipate that the work would eventually disseminate the term *magical realism* around the world, just as the wind blows seeds in all directions. In the 1960s, the Latin American boom began to draw global attention to literature from this "miracle" region, and in addition to García Márquez's *One Hundred Years of Solitude*, the Boom included works like Carlos Fuentes's *The Death of Artemio Cruz*, Mario Vargas Llosa's *The Time of the Hero*, and Julio Cortázar's *Hopscotch*. What people today discuss the most, however, is still García Márquez and his *One Hundred Years of Solitude*. This is literature, but literature is also a kind of history, and there isn't only one literary history. History always wants to remember the victors while ignoring those who struggled unsuccessfully along the same path, and although the result is perhaps somewhat cruel, it is also inevitable. At least in China, this is how literature and history work.

Three decades ago, *One Hundred Years of Solitude* was as popular in China as Michael Jackson's songs, and to read the novel and fail to discuss García Márquez's magical realism would have been like entering a movie theatre without purchasing a ticket. Even today, after countless other twentieth-century literary trends have already faded from view, *One Hundred Years of Solitude* continues to be widely embraced. If we treat the novel as evidence of our understanding of literature or of a certain literary concept, we can begin by asking what it is about the novel and magical realism that most often comes to mind. For instance, some of the novel's most-discussed unbelievable plotlines include:

1 A child is born with a pig's tail.
2 A girl develops a habit of eating earth with lime from the walls of her house.
3 People are unable to defeat vines.
4 People collectively forget important events.
5 One character's false teeth sprout aquatic plants with yellow flowers.
6 A character goes mad and ends up being tied to a chestnut tree for years.
7 A small crib is constantly flying away.
8 A character deliberately places her hand on burning coals, after which she wraps the injured hand in a black bandage.

Even after we finish reading the novel, these miraculous, mysterious, and magical plots continue to linger in our imagination. Although we can't say that these plots are examples of magical realism, at least we can say that they gave us our first impression of magical realism. Just as someone stumbling on a seemingly familiar road may notice certain differences between this road and the one that he takes every day, we similarly cannot say for certain that these sorts of plots are truly unprecedented but rather simply that they had never before been so concentrated in a single work. In fact, we could even say that it is precisely these strange and unusual plots that are responsible for the novel's greatness.

An issue that readers up to now have overlooked and therefore have not pursued is that virtually all plotlines like the ones in the preceding list—which are not only ubiquitous in *One Hundred Years of Solitude* itself but also permeate the empty spaces between the lines of the novel—feature impossible occurrences. Although García Márquez used this sort of "impossibility" to create his novel, we as readers have not yet investigated these plotlines' causal impossibility, incompleteness, and nonequivalence.

In other words, the novel is not grounded in the sort of full causality that we find in conventional realism. However, rather than pursuing a full investigation of the rationality of the logic of stories, plots, and characters that transcends full causality's conception of what is "possible," we instead simply respond with a knowing smile. No reader or critic would ask questions like: How could a child be born with a pig's tail? What is the fundamental reason for the tail's existence? What kind of cause could account for this sort of result? Does the result have an enabling condition? If so, is it reasonable and fair? Is the relationship between cause and result equal to the relationship between half a pound and eight ounces? Why, in other words, are we so much more tolerant of García Márquez's causal logic than we are of Kafka's?

Consider the following passages from the opening paragraphs of each author's respective magnum opus. As we have noted, *The Metamorphosis* famously opens with this description:

As Gregor Samsa awoke one morning from uneasy dreams he found himself transformed in his bed into a gigantic insect. He was lying on his hard, as it were armor-plated, back and when he lifted his head a little he could see his domelike brown belly divided into stiff arched segments on top of which the bed quilt could hardly keep in position and was about to slide off completely. His numerous legs, which were pitifully thin compared to the rest of his bulk, waved helplessly before his eyes.[1]

Meanwhile, the opening of *One Hundred Years of Solitude* features this description:

Every year during the month of March a family of ragged gypsies would set up their tents near the village, and with a great uproar of pipes and kettledrums they would display new inventions. First they brought the magnet. A heavy gypsy with an untamed beard and sparrow hands, who introduced himself as Melquíades, put on a bold public demonstration of what he himself called the eighth wonder of the learned alchemists of Macedonia. He went from house to house dragging two metal ingots and everybody was amazed to see pots, pans, tongs, and braziers tumble down from their places and beams creak from the desperation of nails and screws trying to emerge, and even objects that had been lost for a long time appeared from where they had been searched for most and went dragging along in turbulent confusion behind Melquíades' magical irons.[2]

Regardless of whether we compare these passages directly, recall our original reaction when we first read the works, or simply consider how we remember them now—we must admit that although we may doubt the plausibility of Gregor Samsa's overnight transformation into an insect, we certainly don't question the plausibility of Melquíades dragging around a pair of magnets that are able to pull down every home's pots, pans, tongs, and braziers. The former does not give readers a sense of plausibility, while the latter appears eminently possible.

In other words, the former begins and develops from a space of impossibility, while the latter develops from a space of possibility.

In the first case, the work has no need to acknowledge the reader's existence, meaning that it can break away from full causality and permit its characters and story to originate from a space of zero causality. In the second case, by contrast, we find a causality that is neither full nor zero causality. This new causality is greater than (or less than) the completeness and equivalence of full causality—because of the inherent plausibility of the causal relationship between magnets and iron, readers are therefore not inclined to be too skeptical of this fictional scenario in which long-lost iron implements suddenly emerge when a magnet passes by. Readers might consciously recognize that a magnet is incapable of making the nails and screws embedded in wooden beams and furniture noisily struggle to work themselves loose. However, even if the cause is inferior (or superior) to the result, or if the result is inferior (or superior) to the cause, and even if there is a lack of equivalence between the proportion, weight, volume, and energy of the magnets and the iron implements, no reader would doubt the underlying logic of their relationship. This is because the cause and result are linked neither by full causality nor by zero causality, and instead by what we could call partial causality.

We use *partial causality* to refer to this relationship that exists but is fundamentally incommensurate. Partial causality is less than full causality yet greater than zero causality, and it circulates in the space between the two. This partial causality is precisely the new causality—or potential causality—that García Márquez bequeathed to the world.

Realism's full causality organizes and constructs a story's plot, subplots, and characters, even as it develops and advances the work's trajectory. This is a kind of "necessary possibility," and necessity is the highest standard for the contact and communication of these various elements. Zero causality, by contrast, rejects this sort of necessity, and its contribution to fiction is instead an "impossible" causality. However, García Márquez discovered a sort of "seemingly possible" that functions as an intermediary between the possible and the impossible. Authors must be firm and resolute in their approach to fictional causality, and regardless of whether they are attempting to conform to full causality or to zero causality, their position with respect to writing's causal relations must be similarly clear and unambiguous.

"All happy families are alike but an unhappy family is unhappy after its own fashion."[3] After proposing this thesis at the beginning of *Anna Karenina*, Tolstoy proceeded to demonstrate its correctness by discussing at length the reasons why families are or are not happy. Under full causality, authors must always devote an enormous effort to demonstrating the fundamental irrefutability of their conclusions, and they will maintain a faithful attitude toward this kind of necessary causality, thereby demonstrating its legitimacy. For instance, the cunning, greedy, and stingy Eugénie Grandet, in Balzac's eponymous novel, is a paradigmatic example of such a protagonist, and Balzac never permits us to suspect that there might be any fault in the causality in which he is grounded. Jean Valjean in Hugo's *Les Misérables* is astonishing and Quasimodo in *The Hunchback of Notre Dame* is legendary—yet as characters they both appear completely reasonable and reliable.

In Kafka, meanwhile, we find courageous pursuit of noncausality and irrationality that resembles the careful manner in which Tolstoy had Anna Karenina suddenly stop loving her husband Karenin after she noticed that his ears were ugly. The absurdity of K's inability to enter the castle and Joseph K's repeated arrests and interrogations cannot be explained by a conventional logic of $1 + 1 = 2$. Like Tolstoy's commitment to full causality, Kafka's resistance to and betrayal of rationality displays a distinctive all-or-nothing attitude. Although each author's attitude toward the result in each case might appear very different, both are actually firm and resolute in their approach. By García Márquez's era, however, this kind of resoluteness had disappeared and been replaced by murkiness. As a result, a Márquezian "seemingly possible" wanders within a virtual space located between a Tolstoyian "completely possible" and Kafkaesque "completely impossible."

For instance, after José Acadio II, in *One Hundred Years of Solitude*, was shot to death, blood from his wound gushed like a river into the street, then "continued on in a straight line across the uneven terraces, went down steps and climbed over curbs, passed along the street of the Turks, turned a corner to the right and another to the left, made a right and another to the left, made a right angle at the Buendía house," where it reported José Acadio's unfortunate death to his family.[4] Here, the "cause" is the flowing blood, while the "result" is that not only can the blood orient itself in the correct direction, it can even climb stairs and flow into the house of the deceased. Obviously, the result is vastly greater than the underlying cause, but there are still the additional factors of the reality of flowing blood and the local folk culture of "a spirit returning home." As for a child being born with a pig's tail, it is true that at an earlier stage in the evolutionary process, the ancestors of modern humans were in fact born with tails. For years after Melquíades's death he is able to return to his former room in the Buendía house and speak to people, while Colonel Aureliano Buendía, in his old age, spends every day in his room fashioning tiny goldfish out of gold foil. García Márquez's novel is filled with these sorts of "possible yet impossible" causal relations, which create a magical miracle. This causality is grounded in a combination of traditional culture and Latin American reality, but the plot features elements that, based to the principles of everyday reality, would normally appear to be completely impossible. The surprising plotlines and accidents involve things that do not exist in everyday life, though they may contain traces of "absolute reality."

The basic logic of magic realism's partial causality involves a progression from a small (or extremely small) cause, to a limited (or unlimited) expansion, to a possible (or impossible) conclusion. If we were to place zero causality, partial causality, and full causality along a single axis, meanwhile, their relationship would be as follows:

full causality   partial causality   zero causality

Full causality and zero causality are both self-contained, while partial causality is suspended between them. Full causality has a pious and loyal attitude, and is willing to expend limitless effort to protect the legitimacy of its causality—to the point of going to extraordinary lengths to prove where it has come from, even retracing the entire route it has just traversed. By contrast, zero causality only reveals the direction from which it has come and doesn't care whether you believe it or not—thereby leaving readers with a feeling of separation and coldness. Partial causality, meanwhile, tells you that it has arrived from that distant location, but if you don't believe it, it won't go back and retrace its steps; instead, it will simply smile mysteriously, take out a leaf or branch picked up from the route it has just traversed, and offer it as evidence. Sometimes that leaf or branch might strike you as familiar, but other times it will appear completely unfamiliar and you'll have no idea whether this evidence is real.

There is a character in *One Hundred Years of Solitude* who likes to eat dirt, and although readers may be skeptical of this, they nevertheless will certainly have heard of someone in real life who eats dirt. The novel also claims that the most powerful living thing is a vine, and when humans try to fight vines they will inevitably lose. Although you may view this claim with skepticism, you too will have had the experience of cutting down a vine one day, only to see it grow back the next.

Partial causality is based on the reality that it presents, but it is never completely cut off from everyday life. When partial causality presents its own reality, it does not exaggerate that reality and instead attempts to minimize it. It would never be completely loyal to that reality—which is to say, it would never act like a camera, where the image that appears in the lens is directly determined by the reality outside. It is as though, on the axis of causality, partial causality has a pulley that is controlled by the author. This way, whenever partial causality begins to approach full causality, becoming the sort of reality we observe in everyday life, it is quickly pulled back in the direction of zero causality; and whenever it begins to approach zero causality, becoming something that could not possibly occur in real life, it is pulled back in the direction of full causality. Partial causality is therefore like an adolescent perched on a half-real and half-illusory skateboard, dancing between innocent youth and mature adulthood. To readers, this adolescent's face will not appear old and wise, but neither will it appear cold and distant. Instead, the face draws on the strength of both and assumes its own form, becoming warm, kind, and filled with an unruly lovability. Although we cannot say that partial causality is fully believable and necessary, neither can we say that it is completely unbelievable and impossible. The resulting indeterminacy wins over many readers and critics, as a result of which they take their love for Tolstoy's full causality and their astonishment for Kafka's zero causality and transfer them over to García Márquez's partial causality.

3 A SECOND ATTITUDE TOWARD PARTIAL CAUSALITY

It is often said that if someone likes Tolstoy, Balzac, and Flaubert, they usually won't be able to accept Kafka; and conversely if they idolize Kafka, they usually won't be inclined to turn around and praise those earlier realist authors. Although the latter readers may offer testimonials praising works by the great realist authors, this is more a function of their respect for literary history than any true affinity for the realist works themselves.

Miraculously, García Márquez was able to bring together these stubborn realists and the readers who expressed delighted astonishment at Kafka's zero causality, allowing both groups to set aside their prejudices and join together in enjoying his own works. Particularly in the eyes of Chinese authors and readers, this was truly an incredible achievement comparable to building a bridge between two beloved two mountain peaks, and just as each peak had its own distinct scenery before the bridge was completed, zero causality and full causality were also diametrically opposed, with each group of authors having a completely different view of reality and the world and creating completely different realities in their writings. However, when García Márquez developed partial causality, he succeeded in reconciling these two distinct understandings of reality and the world and was thereby able to retain readers interested in zero causality while bringing back those who preferred full causality. García Márquez's readers were positioned between these two previously opposed groups, meaning that they were able to embrace his literature's strange, new, and unique magical power while enjoying its broad recognition. The reason García Márquez was able to enjoy such success is because, in addition to offering partial causality as a middle path between full and zero causality, he simultaneously offered a return to the type of society and characters that were foregrounded in nineteenth-century literature. It is thanks to him that twentieth-century fiction partially recovered from its earlier tendency to downplay society and characters.

Whereas the preceding discussion has focused on the question of "how to write," the question of "what to write" was also undergoing a remarkable transformation during this same period. Full causality's attitude toward reality and the world is critical, interventionist, and expansive, and nearly all its fictional characters are actually social figures. The stories are driven by an uneasy oscillation between social relations and real life. It was not only Anna Karenina's emotions and personality that impelled her to throw herself under the train, but also the transformative moment in nineteenth-century Russia in which she lived, in which "everything has been turned upside down and is only just taking shape."[5] Similarly, although Katyusha Maslova's tragic fate in The Resurrection was partially due to her nature, the real culprit was the dark and complicated Russian social reality in which she lived. In his preface to La Comédie Humaine, Balzac observed that his objective was "to complete a work that describes nineteenth-century France," just as the original subtitle of Stendhal's The Red and the Black was "A Chronicle of the Nineteenth Century" and the original subtitle of Flaubert's Madame Bovary was "Provincial Manners."

All these great realist works convey the intimate relationship between full-causal writing and the contradictions inherent in the author's own society. For instance, although in Madame Bovary Emma Rouault was a rural woman from the outer provinces and although Flaubert primarily offers detailed descriptions of scenes outside Paris, he nevertheless doesn't neglect to describe how, when Emma was at the convent, she encountered an old woman who is identified as belonging "to an ancient family of noblemen ruined by the Revolution," not to mention the fact that the novel's historical background was France during the era of the

House of Bourbon.[6] In the end, Flaubert was writing not only about France's outer provinces but also about that society's most important composition, and in this way his work offered a maximum presentation of real society and the world at the time.

In full-causal realist writing, the attempt to make social contradictions deeper and more complex relies on a process of rational assimilation whereby the more fully rendered the characters are, the more moving the work will be. In zero-causal writing, by contrast, a strong social background is no longer the stage on which characters and stories are developed. Social figures become instead individuals. We find the same phenomenon in these works' treatment of death. For instance, in *Anna Karenina* the protagonist is driven to kill herself by the complexity of the society in which she lived, while in Kafka's story "The Judgement" the protagonist Georg Bendermann jumps into the river simply because of his father's pronouncement: "Understand this: I sentence you now to death by drowning!"[7] In *The Metamorphosis*, meanwhile, no reason at all is given for why Gregor Samsa becomes an insect, or for why his father subsequently throws the apple that becomes lodged in his back and kills him. In *The Castle* the protagonist K leaves the kind of household environment in which Georg Bendermann found himself in "The Judgement" and arrives in a village located at the base of a castle. Regardless of whether this village corresponds to a real-life location or is a purely fictional site, it is larger than a household yet is hardly the sort of complex social environment that we typically find in full-causal novels. Instead, the village has a mysterious symbolic existence, in contrast to the sort of social existence we would expect to find in realist fiction. By the time we get to *The Trial*, meanwhile, the story's trajectory and society have entered into a complex correspondence with one another, as the work focuses primarily on the correlation between a specific society and the law, which cannot be compared to the comprehensive social relations that we find in works by critical realist authors.

Indeed, full causality is committed to detailing the causal relations between society and characters' lives. One of the objectives of full-causal works is to illustrate and critique social complexity, and it is precisely this objective that is betrayed by zero causality. Zero causality severs the direct relationship between characters and society such that the work's only connection with grand historical background becomes merely symbolic, reliant on reader's own associations. Full causality's creation of complex characters also becomes an objective—and even the sole objective—of realism in post–zero-causal modernist writing, even as the simplified stories become increasingly bizarre and their characters are reduced to mere symbols. Therefore, readers who like full causality and who view zero causality with a mixture of incomprehension and apprehension will become increasingly silent and reserved. Conversely, readers who support modernist writing will have no choice but to express their respect for those great authors working in the tradition of full causality and express their disdain for those who vow their undying loyalty to full-causal writing. Full-causal and zero-causal writing constitute two completely independent camps. The enormous global readership that nineteenth-century literature cultivated was not very receptive to zero causality, the same way an old person might not particularly like the changes the modern world has undergone. Meanwhile, modernist readers and authors cultivated in the twentieth century do not deny the greatness of nineteenth-century literature, though they may regard that kind of full-causal writing with a certain degree of disdain.

By García Márquez's time, this kind of contradiction was finally resolved, such that those authors and readers who worshipped zero causality were able to appreciate his development of zero causality, while those who worshipped full causality could appreciate the way he inherited and reinvented full causality. The partial causality deployed throughout *One Hundred Years of Solitude* reveals García Márquez's attitude toward reality and history, and constitutes a kind of return and redemption. Unlike authors in the modernist tradition, García Márquez did not focus solely on individual characters to the exclusion of society and history and instead approached fiction by relying on stories and characters that were created under the banner of literature but that actually belonged to the real world.

In full-causal writing, fictional characters and the historical environment are rich and complex, while in zero-causal writing, they are comparatively simple and clear—though the inner world of individual characters in the latter remains rich and complex. With partial causality, meanwhile, García Márquez effectively combined both approaches. He retreated half a step from Kafka's betrayal of full causality, and then, tugging at zero causality with one hand and at full causality with the other, he collected the aspects of stories, characters, and modern society that zero causality had discarded, and strove to reincorporate them into his fiction.

In other words, compared to modernist authors after Kafka, García Márquez displayed a deep affection for and attention to the relationship between stories and characters, as well as to the social and historical realities to which readers normally attend. For instance, *One Hundred Years of Solitude* follows the miraculous history of seven generations of the Buendía clan, together with the century-long history of the fictional town of Macondo—from its initial rise, development, and prosperity to its eventual fall. In this way, García Márquez was able to describe the parallel historical development of Colombia and of all Latin America. When the Swedish Royal Academy awarded García Márquez the Nobel Prize for Literature in 1992, it cited the way "the fantastic and the realistic are combined in a richly composed world of imagination."[8] Here, "the fantastic" refers to the widespread and perfect use of partial causality in *One Hundred Years of Solitude*, while "the realistic" refers to García Márquez's return to society and reality following his deep attention to his people's reality and history.

It is impossible to say for certain whether it was the Nobel Prize that granted *One Hundred Years of Solitude* its current canonical status, or whether it was instead García Márquez's literary achievement that further consolidated the prize's own global reputation. Either way, it is clear that from the moment García Márquez won the prize, Latin American literature was no longer oriented solely toward Latin America, or even just to the rest of the Western world. The accolade allowed enlightened authors and readers to realized that to focus on a novel's characters as individuals is a glorious trap, while to focus only on their position within society could incite a momentary uproar followed by a deafening silence. Fellow Latin American authors such as Vargas Llosa, Fuentes, and Cortázar did not abandon their interest in history and local reality and instead succeeded in synthesizing the literary experience of the nineteenth and the first half of the twentieth century. And even if these authors weren't consciously thinking in these terms, the gods must have been secretly supporting them and prodding them along. If García Márquez had never written this fictional history of his people's century-long trajectory and had never created such vivid characters, and if his work had instead only featured an assortment of miraculous and magical elements, would it still have achieved the same level of greatness?

4   APPROACHES TO PARTIAL CAUSALITY (3)

Full-causal novels, regardless of their objective, must constantly attempt to display the historical setting inhabited by their characters, together with the complex contradictions that characterize the relationship between characters and society. As a zero-causal author, however, Kafka rejected this sort of approach, and instead his novels are a fictional product of a confusion of author and characters, compounded by a latent social entanglement. Our desire to express our engagement with and understanding of Kafka's mysterious works is undermined by the works' own black hole of meaning, and the author's abstract yet engaging use of language is a virtual gaze that draws readers to this figurative black hole of meaning. In this way, he incorporates into his fiction our own contradictory understandings of the relationship between individuals and society. Furthermore, if Kafka incorporates enough of this understanding into his works, it will confirm that our understanding of those same works is sufficiently deep.

Realism is realism as read by readers.

Modernism is modernism as allegorized and mythologized by readers.

Kafka is one of the authors who most easily lends himself to being allegorized and mythologized, while in García Márquez's "semi-causal" writings the author, history, and the construction of reality have a more direct and subtle existence. Balzac, Flaubert, Hugo, Tolstoy, and Turgenev all used their writing to develop the contradictions between authors, characters, and society. Their works, accordingly, are readers' novels, in that all that readers need to do is to feel and experience them. Kafka's works, by contrast, belong to the author himself, and his readers must struggle to reflect on them. Most of the time that process does not allow readers to follow the same path as the author but rather relies on the readers' own exploration. This is also one of the reasons why reading Kafka is so much more exhausting than reading Tolstoy. However, when reading *One Hundred Years of Solitude*, we adopt a relaxed and idiosyncratic appreciation of how a historical and social reality is developed through the story and its characters.

García Márquez's literature is perceived as being realistic precisely because it is the product of the author's choices and filters, and these choices and filters reflect the attitude with which the author approaches history. Tolstoy attempted to use a full-causal approach to display and critique nineteenth-century Russia's history of social change, in which "everything has been turned upside down and is only just taking shape." Meanwhile, Kafka's approach to his own era consisted of a self-doubting "noncausal" display of a kind of Jewish culture. Self-doubt resulted in "noncause," just as the "noncause" in his works displays even more deeply this Jewish historical culture. When García Márquez confronts the relationship between history and the characters and stories in *One Hundred Years of Solitude*, his approach is informed both by a commitment to realism and by a rejection of modernism.

While works by full-causal authors reflect a commitment to history and reality, in *The Metamorphosis*, *The Castle*, and *The Trial*, by contrast, Kafka approaches his people's history with an attitude that, if not a complete rejection, at the very least quietly shifts its historical focus toward local Jewish culture. Kafka used local Jewish reality to replace the focus on history and the intricate relationships between individual and society that traditional authors typically incorporate into their novels, thereby giving his readers the impression that conventional descriptions of society and history had been transferred to a secular narrative environment that was resistant to reason. If readers of novels like *The Metamorphosis* and *The Castle* hope to experience society and history as they would when reading nineteenth-century novels, they will surely be deeply disappointed. García Márquez's readers, meanwhile, are unable to find either realism's full causality or modernism's zero causality. They are unable to appreciate Tolstoy's efforts to display and critique social reality and local history, and they are similarly unable to appreciate Kafka's display of a shift of history and social realities toward local Jewish culture. Instead, all they can find is a fictional depiction of a hidden social relationship.

García Márquez did not avoid engaging the history and reality of his people. In this respect, his approach is not unlike what we find in realism. The key difference between García Márquez's work and traditional realism, however, is that García Márquez uses a highly individualized historical attitude—a kind of semi-causal attitude informed by individual aesthetics. When realist authors approach history and complex social reality, by contrast, they almost invariably seek to discover, reveal, and critique. Because they discover, they reveal; because they reveal, they critique; and because they critique, they therefore become great. Because these authors critique, future generations will confirm their greatness. In nineteenth-century realist novels, accordingly, history and society are greater than fictional characters and determine the characters' lives. A character may attempt to resist reality and history, but as a social being, he or she is inevitably a "social figure" and therefore a part of society. García Márquez, by contrast, incorporates partial causality into his approach to society and history. In his works, stories and characters join society and are unable to get away from local history. However, history and society are not greater than the fictional characters, and the characters' fate lies in the semi-causal individual rather than in a complex social causality. Society is "people's society," but people are not necessarily "society's people." This is a fundamental difference between traditional realism and García Márquez's fiction. In the former, characters develop out of social history; in the latter, history and society develop out of characters.

In *One Hundred Years of Solitude*, Colonel Aureliano Buendía not only participates in society and history, he also actively creates Macondo's local history. Throughout his life he strives to conquer the world, launching thirty-two failed rebellions. However, these insurrections are not like nineteenth-century heroes struggling on behalf of nation, society, and true democracy and freedom, but rather they are simply launched on behalf of his masculine pride. The colonel acts not to pursue social advancement, nor to seize power in order to control the world, but rather his actions, as thrilling and indomitable as they may have been, are ultimately simply for the sake of his masculine pride. In realistic terms this diminishes the novel's historical significance, but in aesthetic terms it elevates and enriches the artistry of the story's characters (and, by extension, of the characters' historicity).

Consider, for instance, the following description of Colonel Aureliano Buendía's relationship to his brother:

Years later, when Colonel Aureliano Buendía examined the titles to property, he found registered in his brother's name all of the land between the hill where his yard was on up to the horizon, including the cemetery, and discovered that during the eleven months of his rule, Arcadio had collected not only the money of the contributions, but had also collected fees from people for the right to bury their dead in José Arcadio's land.[9]

This is one of the novel's more socially significant descriptions, and it reveals how the Buendía clan, like society itself, was characterized by a combination of power and corruption. However, García Márquez deliberately downplayed this element of social critique and instead simply used the description of the brother's greed to develop his fictional character. Furthermore, the author does not devote very much attention to this sort of description, and he certainly does not use it to endow society and history with some sort of grand significance. The significance of the novel's characters exceeds that of society and history—this is the attitude with which *One Hundred Years of Solitude* approaches society and history. Given Latin America's long history of being a colonial territory, this marks an important turning point. The reality of the oppression and persecution that people endured under colonialism is a history of blood and tears that all realist fiction must address, but under García Márquez's pen this history only appears in a semiobscured manner, as in the following passage:

> During that time a brother of the forgotten Colonel Magnífico Visbal was taking his seven-year-old grandson to get a soft drink at one of the pushcarts on the square and because the child accidentally bumped into a corporal of police and spilled the drink on his uniform, the barbarian cut him to pieces with his machete, and with one stroke he cut off the head of the grandfather as he tried to stop him. The whole town saw the decapitated man pass by as a group of men carried him to his house, with a woman dragging the head along by its hair, and the bloody sack with the pieces of the child.[10]

This passage is not so much a representation of colonial oppression as it is an illustration of how the author uses his semi-causal literary perspective to view history and reality. We can observe two causal sequences in this passage. First, the child's drink spills on the officer's uniform, which leads the officer to chop the child to pieces. Second, the officer chops off the head of a grandfather who tries to stop him, whereupon a woman grabs the severed head by the hair and drags it away. In the first case a seemingly insignificant cause results in a portentous result, while in the second a portentous cause yields an extremely mundane result. García Márquez did not avoid history and reality. However, he did not attempt to transform complex social contradictions into hidden social relations, as Kafka did, but neither did he attempt to use a moral perspective to reveal and critique them, as realist authors did. Instead, he strove to remove morality from reality, leaving behind only his own narration and the semi-causal relationships with which he approaches these exaggerated or diminished characters and their corresponding social contradictions.

The new relationship between authors, history, and social reality that *Hundred Years of Solitude* offered twentieth-century literature lies in the way the novel let history and social reality return to stories that are grounded in the individual, thereby recovering the society and history that had disappeared from Kafkaesque modernist fiction, while simultaneously avoiding the dominant position they had previously enjoyed in realist fiction. History and social reality were similarly selected and filtered by partial causality, and the resulting characters and minor characters are all incorporated into García Márquez's semi-causal literary method and world view. This, in turn, is the new relationship between author, history, and social reality that *One Hundred Years of Solitude* offered twentieth-century literature.

5   THE SOURCES OF PARTIAL CAUSALITY (1)

The global explosion of semi-causal writing after the mid-twentieth century was not limited to García Márquez and Latin American literature. Novels like Joseph Heller's *Catch-22*, Camus's *The Plague*, Thomas Pynchon's *Gravity's Rainbow*, Günter Grass's *The Tin Drum*, and works by the Beat Generation all contain semi-causal elements, and even a work like Orwell's *1984* features no shortage of semi-causal techniques. The differences between the semi-causal techniques in these works simply come down to questions of amount, frequency, proficiency, and whether these techniques are used consciously or unconsciously.

Without question, García Márquez thought carefully about how to develop partial causality, and it is thanks to him that partial causality was elevated from mere technique to a way of understanding the world. In examining the relationship between partial and zero causality, many readers will be reminded of the astonishment and excitement they felt upon first reading Kafka, and this is described very clearly in García Márquez's biography, *Journey Back to the Source*.[11] In García Márquez's most important works, however, it is difficult to find a direct manifestation of Kafka's zero causality. Why is this? In *The Fragrance of Guava*, García Márquez's dialogue with fellow Columbian author Plineo Apuleyo Mendoza, García Márquez discussed his relationship to Kafka and the mode of literary creation that Kafka represents:

> *Was it through your grandmother that you discovered you were going to be a writer?*
>
> No, it was through Kafka, who recounted things in German, the same way my grandmother used to. When I read *The Metamorphosis*, at seventeen, I realized I could be a writer. When I saw how Gregor Samsa could wake up on morning transformed into a gigantic beetle, I said to myself, "I didn't know you could do this, but if you can, I'm certainly interested in writing."
>
> *Why did it attract you so strongly? Because of the freedom of being able to invent anything you like?*
>
> All of a sudden I understood how many other possibilities existed in literature outside the rational and extremely academic examples I'd come across in secondary school text books. It was like tearing off a chastity belt. Over the years, however, I discovered that you can't invent or imagine just whatever you fancy because then you risk not telling the truth and lies are more serious in literature than in real life. Even the most seemingly arbitrary creation has its rules. You can throw away the fig leaf of rationalism only if you don't then descend into total chaos and irrationality.
>
> *Into fantasy?*
>
> Yes, into fantasy.
>
> *You loathe fantasy. Why?*
>
> Because I believe the imagination is just an instrument for producing reality and that the source of creation is always, in the last instance, reality. Fantasy, in the sense of pure and simple Walt-Disney-style invention without any basis in reality is the most loathsome thing of all.[12]

Here, García Márquez addresses three issues:

1   The inspirational influence that *The Metamorphosis* had on him. As Mendoza describes elsewhere in the text:

> When [García Márquez] finished secondary school and began studying law at the National University of Bogota, poetry continued to be his main interest in life.... His interest in the novel began the night he read Kafka's *The Metamorphosis*. He now recalls how he arrived back at his miserable student hostel in the center of town, clutching this book which a fellow student had just lent him. He took his jacket and shoes off, lay on his bed, opened the book and read: "As Gregor Samsa awoke one morning from uneasy dreams, he found himself transformed in his bed into a gigantic insect." Gabriel closed the book, trembling. "Christ," he thought, "so this is what you can do." The next day he wrote his first short story. He forgot about his studies.[13]

2   Over time, García Márquez's understanding of writing matured as he came to realize that "you can't invent or imagine just whatever you fancy" and developed a strong aversion to pure fantasy.

3   The source of imagination is always reality, or, as García Márquez puts it, "every good novel should be a poetic transcription of reality."[14]

This is a case of one great author inspiring another, even though the latter may have remained somewhat skeptical of the former. An author who doesn't respect another's creativity is exhibiting a kind of ignorance, but an author who isn't skeptical of his or her seniors is also useless. We don't know when or under what circumstances García Márquez concluded that Kafka's writing was a simply a product of his pure fantasy, nor is there any need for us to know this. However, his skepticism toward zero causality and rationalism was unmistakable: "You can throw away the fig leaf of rationalism only if you don't then descend into total chaos and irrationality." If this characterization of writing's rationalism as a kind of virtual fig leaf doesn't reflect García Márquez's aversion to zero-causal writing, it is at the very least evidence of his hatred of illogic. Even so, in retreating from this illogical zero causality, García Márquez did not return to a completely logical full causality.

"I've never read anything of [Tolstoy's]," García Márquez declared without any hesitation, though he simultaneously conceded that *War and Peace* is "the best novel ever written."[15] With this pair of statements, it is not difficult to observe that García Márquez developed partial causality because he looked down on Tolstoy's full causality but simultaneously didn't approve of Kafka's zero causality. He didn't embrace full causality, but also couldn't help acknowledging that *War and Peace* is the best novel ever written. Conversely, he hated Kafka's pure fantasy, but had to recognize the inspiration he himself derived from Kafka's zero causality. Therefore, García Márquez ultimately positioned himself in an interstitial region between Kafka and Tolstoy where he could avoid not only a "Gregor Samsa awoke one morning from uneasy dreams" kind of illogical fantasy, but also an overly traditional full-causal logic such as Anna Karenina's disgust at how her husband's ears struck her "pressing up against the brim of his round hat."[16] In this way, partial causality was born—not only as a writing technique, but also as a way of understanding the world.

6 THE SOURCES OF PARTIAL CAUSALITY (2)

García Márquez may have hated Kafka's empty fantasy, and in his dialogue with Mendoza he spoke approvingly of other authors such as Ernest Hemingway, William Faulkner, Arthur Rimbaud, and the Spanish Golden Age poets. In fact, at one point he even admitted that he composed his favorite short story, "Tuesday Siesta," after reading Hemingway's "A Canary for One." However, if we consider García Márquez's oeuvre from the perspective of partial causality, then Kafka's zero causality must be regarded as the true original source. We could take as examples García Márquez's two early short stories, "Eyes of a Blue Dog" and "Nabo, the Black Man Who Made the Angels Wait." The former describes a man who, in his dreams, repeatedly encounters a woman with whom he is infatuated because everywhere she goes, she continually repeats and writes the same mysterious phrase: "Eyes of a Blue Dog."[17] The latter, meanwhile, describes how the eponymous protagonist was kicked in the forehead while trying to groom a horse's tail, which left him paralyzed for fifteen years. For those fifteen years a mute girl constantly sat by his side while listening to a gramophone, until eventually one day, "after they'd fastened the door again, they heard the difficult movements inside once more.... Inside something like the panting of a penned animal was heard." The black man rushed out of the room like a wild animal, but when the mute girl who had cared for him for fifteen years saw him, she "remembered the only word she had ever learned to say in her life, and shouted it from the living room: 'Nabo! Nabo!'"[18]

Both these love stories contain zero-causal elements inspired by *The Metamorphosis*. Who is the woman who appears in the man's dreams and continually repeats the phrase *eyes of a blue dog*? Why does she always appear in someone else's dreams? And what does the phrase *eyes of a blue dog* even mean? García Márquez doesn't address any of these questions, which is also a transplant of Kafka's hegemonic narration. Similarly, after Nabo was kicked in the forehead, he spent fifteen years in a coma while the mute girl kept watch over him. Nabo spent those fifteen years locked in his room like Gregor Samsa after being transformed into an insect—the only difference being that after Samsa's transformation, his family and others began to distance themselves from him, while Nabo had the mute girl to watch over him during his insect-like existence following the accident. But can someone really lie in the same room for fifteen years? From the perspective of full causality, the room should have developed a corpse-like stench, and in fact we are told that after Nabo woke up, he resembled "a blindfolded bull in a roomful of lamps ... [he] reached the back yard (still without finding the stable), and scratched on the ground with the tempestuous fury with which he had knocked down the mirror, thinking perhaps that by scratching on the ground he could make the smell of mare's urine rise up again, until he finally reached the stable doors."[19]

Based solely on these two stories, we may conclude that the issue is not so much that there was a close connection between the absurdist logic found in García Márquez's and Kafka's works, but rather that the logic with which García Márquez perceived the world was borrowed from Kafka's zero causality. These early stories are not necessarily García Márquez's best works, but without them he might not have composed some of his later works like "One Day after Saturday."

In "One Day after Saturday" García Márquez wrote about Latin America's "miraculous reality"—namely, an incident in which a large flock of birds mysteriously kill themselves. A flock of birds committing suicide like a pod of whales draws on one of the distinguishing qualities associated with humans, and the scenario has its own internal logical causality and necessity. This is not a groundless event, like a person becoming an insect, and therefore readers are invited to view it with a combination of belief and skepticism—yielding a new causality that is distinct from both full causality and zero causality. When partial causality emerged in García Márquez's fiction it was like the sun rising out of the mist, and after the success of works like "One Day after Saturday" this virtual sun finally reached its zenith in *One Hundred Years of Solitude*.

What is even more interesting is that although García Márquez was somewhat bored with Kafka's empty fantasy (zero causality), he nevertheless enthusiastically praised Graham Greene's works, saying,

> Yes, Graham Greene taught me how to decipher the tropics, no less. To separate out the essential elements of a poetic synthesis from an environment you know all too well is extremely difficult. It's all so familiar you don't know where to start and yet you have so much to say that you end by understanding nothing.... Some of them fell into the trap of listing things and, paradoxically, the longer the list the more limited their vision seemed. Others, as we know, have succumbed to rhetorical excess. Graham Greene solved this literary problem in a very precise way—with a few disparate elements connected by an inner coherence both subtle and real. Using this method you can reduce the whole enigma of the tropics to the fragrance of rotten guava.[20]

Later, he explains how Greene helped him "to see that in literature reality is not photographic but synthetic and that finding the essential elements of this synthesis is one of the secrets of the art of narration. Graham Greene does it superbly and I learnt the secrets from him. I think it's all too noticeable in some of my books, particularly, *In Evil Hour*."[21]

With respect to how Greene's work helped García Márquez to "decipher the tropics," the most obvious example is Greene's 1940 novel *The Power and the Glory*, which is the only work of Greene's that García Márquez mentions by name in *The Fragrance of Guava*.

To be honest, however, we always have a slight hesitation when we describe Greene as a great author, though we don't hesitate at all when we speak of García Márquez's greatness. If we compare Greene's *The Power and the Glory* and García Márquez's *In Evil Hour*, we could say that the former gives us a deeper sense of the mystery of the tropics, while the latter gives us an impression of partial causality born out of full causality. For instance, *In Evil Hour* describes how mysterious postings begin appearing in the streets of an unidentified village, detailing many of the villagers' sordid secrets. These postings upset the town mayor, the judge, and priest, as well as the villagers themselves. By the end of the work these anonymous postings end up controlling the novel's story, its mood, and everything in the entire town. These postings, accordingly, constitute the mystery of the tropics, but more importantly they mark a transition from zero causality to partial causality. After all, in any community, anonymous writings are a kind of reality pertaining to the connections between people and their real existence. They can emerge from nothing, but there must nevertheless be something that can possibly exist and not something zero-causal that cannot exist. They also have a zero-causal factor, which is why, when García Márquez said that in writing *In Evil Hour* he took inspiration from Greene's *The Power and the Glory*, what we observe even more clearly is how he was influenced by a logic of zero causality. This is possibly a form of misreading, or perhaps García Márquez once again inadvertently revealed Kafka's influence on him. The reason I say inadvertently revealed is because García Márquez's works give unusual attention to the story's semi-causal relations, but he has never explicitly discussed the relationship between his partial causality and zero or full causality.

García Márquez never discussed his views on causality in his novels, the same way that starving people don't discuss their need for food. However, although starvation feels the same to everyone, there are countless different ways in which starving people experience hunger. When writing fiction, every author must consider the causal relations between one event and another, but precisely because of this everyone must, everyone does, and everyone has—we therefore may overlook this point and not discuss or think about it. Although Kafka and García Márquez never discuss fiction's causality directly, they nevertheless both start from this point and proceed to create new causal logic: namely, zero causality and partial causality, respectively. In this way, they became two pinnacles of twentieth-century literature, the same way that Tolstoy and Balzac were two pinnacles of nineteenth-century fiction. As a result, later authors have no choice but to struggle between full, zero, and partial causality—the same way that we can only plant crops where there is soil, water, and sunlight. Through hard work, we impart the land with love and wisdom, and in return the land gives us crops. We tend to forget, however, that the land is not only our well-being but also our prison—it is the old house filled with the stench of rotting flesh that filled in when Gregor Samsa and Nabo were locked up.

5 Inner Causality

With full, zero, and partial causality serving as a story's soil, water, and sunlight, and after life (which is to say, experience) and inspiration (which is to say, feeling) become the story's seeds, a novel may then begin to germinate. Season after season there will be cultivation and harvest, bumper crops and wipeouts, high seasons and low seasons, good years and bad, and there may even be years in which floods or droughts mean that there is no harvest at all. Through all of this, authors view full causality as a virtual prison in which a story's rules constrain their thought and output and limit their ability to appreciate life. The appearance of zero causality, however, shatters what had been full causality's constraints—whereby a certain cause always had to yield a corresponding result, and a story necessarily featured a direct trajectory from beginning to end. The necessity and equivalence on which full causality relies may lose their efficacy in zero causality, in which a noncause can still yield a result, a result doesn't necessarily require a condition, and a condition doesn't require a possibility (a reason) that readers can personally experience. Stories featuring results without causes offer readers an aesthetic appreciation that is unlike anything that has come before. However, zero causality still betrays the truth contract that authors, readers, and critics have collectively established over millennia, thereby making readers (including García Márquez himself) feel that Kafka's empty fantasy is a betrayal of the sort of life and reality that everyone has personally experienced. It is in this way that partial causality was conceived, and its appearance was linked back to the reality principles of full causality and also ahead to the aesthetic offered by zero causality. From this, a new fictional aesthetic and a "new reality" were conceived, thereby allowing fiction to return to a "simulation" track.

As zero causality and partial causality matured, authors, readers, and critics collectively established—over roughly a century-long period—a new truth contract for fiction: the principle of inner truth.

Inner truth is the truth of people's soul and consciousness, while outer truth is the truth of their behavior and external objects. In twentieth-century modernist writing the struggle to proceed toward truth is, in reality, a struggle to proceed toward inner truth. In nineteenth-century literature, by contrast, we find that all successful works feature a traditional track toward outer truth. In these nineteenth-century works, the transformations of characters' thoughts and souls are driven by (or, at least, are necessarily related to) elements located in the outside world—including society, the environment, and other people. Anna Karenina and Katyusha Maslova, for instance, were miniature reflections of their corresponding era, just as Father Goriot, Eugénie Grandet, and Emma Rouault represented their own eras. Without their historical era, environment, and other people, these fictional characters wouldn't exist. Even for these great characters, their truth penetrates to their life and soul, transcending worldly truth and entering the realm of vital truth and spiritual-depth truth. However, the factors driving characters toward spiritual-depth truth originate from outside, meaning that internal changes originating from outside make fiction proceed from outer truth to inner truth.

In nineteenth-century literature, Raskolnikov is the protagonist with the most inner truth. He possesses the truth of an immortal character's soul and consciousness, though his spiritual conflict, fear, disgust, pride, and denigration all derive from poverty and social injustice. Originally, Tolstoy's display of Raskolnikov's spiritual truth derived not from the author's own soul or from the protagonist's consciousness but rather from an external truth related to his protagonist—namely, Raskolnikov's decision to murder and rob his landlady. This murder and robbery, in turn, derive from Raskolnikov's impoverished state, the concreteness of which is manifested in his inability to pay his debt to his landlady. In the end, everything is driven by a cause, and the reason for that cause is the fuse that is the external world. In other words, it is precisely because there exists an exterior (society) that there therefore also exists an interior (heart and soul). This is also why we call the reality of this "from outside to inside" process of representation a kind of "external truth." This kind of writing is a kind of internalization of external reality, as stories proceed from exteriority to interiority.

After Kafka, however, twentieth-century literature began to follow a trajectory not from exteriority to interiority but rather from interiority to exteriority. If we view Gregor Samsa's transformation into an insect and K's inability to enter the castle as a kind of inner truth, then we notice that each work's original cause is not external to its characters, like the forces that transformed Raskolnikov into a murderer, but instead is disseminated outward from the truth of the characters' inner souls.

Realism emphasizes the materialism of the objective world, while modernism emphasizes the idealism of the subjective world.

Whereas realism transfers stories from outside (society and the environment) to inside (the soul), modernism instead transfers stories from inside to outside. This is the fundamental difference between writing that is oriented toward external truth and that which is oriented toward internal truth. In *The Castle* and *The Trial*, the absurdity of humanity and of the world becomes the source of the story's inner truth, its plotline, and its characters' behavior. These works appear to proceed from inside to outside, but they also contain multiple layers of inner truth. For instance, the more K struggles, the more he is stymied in his attempts to enter the castle, and the resulting focus on the absurdity of humanity, which was previously called expressionism, becomes increasingly prominent. Until the very end of the work the narrative remains focused on the outer truth of K's inability to enter the castle, while in reality the work is actually concerned with inner truth—a more advanced description of the absurdity of humanity and the world.

If we can say that, at the level of inner truth, Kafka has more allegorical and symbolic significance, and presents readers with considerable difficulty when they attempt to decipher his works' significance, then stream-of-consciousness novels can be said to be the ultimate expression of fictional characters' individual consciousness—which is to say, they represent an extreme version of inner-truth writing. In her novel

Mrs. Dalloway, for instance, Virginia Woolf extended her narrative to the interior of her protagonist's mind such that the protagonist's consciousness surges forth like wind in the wilderness. The result is that the character's psychological time breaks through real time and becomes extraordinarily flexible:

> Chill and sharp and yet (for a girl of eighteen as she then was) solemn, feeling as she did, standing there at the open window, that something awful was about to happen; looking at the flowers, at the trees with the smoke winding off them and the rooks rising, falling; standing and looking until Peter Walsh said, "Musing among the vegetables?"— was that it?—"I prefer men to cauliflowers"—was that it? He must have said it at breakfast one morning when she had gone out on to the terrace—Peter Walsh.[1]

This kind of fragmentary, free, and random description of people, be it deliberate or inadvertent, is not simply an innovative literary contribution in the form of stream of consciousness, but it also functions, as Woolf puts it, to "convey this varying, this unknown and uncircumscribed spirit, whatever aberration or complexity it may display, with as little mixture of the alien and external as possible."[2] This inner spirit is precisely the spiritual kernel of inner truth. However, we must concede that after this high point of stream of consciousness during the innovative period of early twentieth-century literature began to fade, during which stream of consciousness was more concrete, realistic, and attuned to protagonist's "internal spirit" than Kafka's internal truth, we realized that we had lost Woolf's great and common experience, which was in contrast to that of the "materialists." From Virginia Woolf's praise of Tolstoy's novel ("There is hardly any subject of human experience that is left out of *War and Peace*"), we can see that she realized the limitations of literature that focuses exclusively on inner spirit.

Today, however, works like *The Metamorphosis* and *The Castle*, as well as classic stream-of-consciousness novels like James Joyce's *Ulysses*, Proust's *Remembrance of Things Past*, and *Mrs. Dalloway*, all demonstrate the literary value of inner truth. Furthermore, because of the appearance of this inner truth, the limits of the outer truth of traditional novels are marked even more clearly.

Once fiction comes to possess inner truth—and regardless of whether this truth is allegorical and symbolic, or detailed and specific—its impact on literature is profound. As readers, we can appreciate that apart from the vast differences in thought, perspective, and technique that separate twentieth-century modernist literature from nineteenth-century realist literature, there is also an essential difference in how authors view reality and the relationship between individuals and society. These two sets of works feature completely different concepts and modes of presentation when it comes to incorporating the relationship between an individual's inner truth and society's outer truth. After inner truth began to appear in modern fiction, several authors developed a mode of "inner causality"—and regardless of whether this inner causality is a true manifestation of the unconscious of the works' fictional characters and stories or is merely a gimmick to make the works more appealing, it subsequently became increasingly ubiquitous within that category of fiction that contains an element of exaggeration.

Inner causality refers to a new logical relationship that is distinct from full, partial, and zero causality. Instead, inner causality involves a set of causes and results that drive the changes in a novel's characters and plot. It is not full causality's elements rooted in the external world (including society, the environment, and other people), nor is it zero causality's murky symbolism and allegory, and even less is it partial causality's odd causal relations hovering in an interstitial space between full and zero causality. Rather, inner causality is based on an inner truth that exists not in real life but rather at the level of the spirit and soul, and it conceives, propels, and extends the changes undergone by stories and fictional characters. In inner-causal fiction, inner truth is the engine that drives the narrative, and it is the only source behind a character's soul and transformation. For instance, in Kafka's famous opening line ("As Gregor Samsa awoke one morning from uneasy dreams he found himself transformed in his bed into a gigantic insect"), this inner truth is the source from which a story develops, and only then will characters be able to speak and act.

Inner truth is fiction's most basic and original condition, without which inner causality would not exist. Literature derived from this foundation of inner truth represents another type of innovative aesthetic production grounded in inner causality. In Joseph Heller's *Catch-22*, for instance, the words and actions of John Yossarian and his fellow soldiers are exaggerated, absurd, and satirical. Each character's actions exceed what we associate with everyday life, but in a "rational" causal relationship the work relies on the same feelings of boredom, fear, and flight that war inspires in everyone. With collective psychology's inner reality, readers can accept the absurd behavior of Yossarian and his fellow soldiers—regardless of whether the characters are on the battlefield, in the market, in a brothel, or in a hospital ward. Works by authors associated with the Beat Generation and authors who practice black humor similarly develop and support the inner truth shared by collectives, society, and human psychology. Without a foundation of inner truth, their novels would resemble buildings with weak foundations, apt to collapse if readers or critics were so much as to spit at or kick them.

The literary value of Orwell's *Animal Farm* is far greater than that of his *1984*. This is not to say that the former is necessarily greater than the latter, but rather that its reflections on power and corruption as they pertain to humanity's collective inner truth have a more timeless and universal significance. There are many other works that share a similar satirical and ironic approach, including Henry Miller's *Tropic of Cancer*, Jack Kerouac's *On the Road*, and Allen Ginsberg's *Howl*, and although from the perspective of outer truth these works are unrealistic in that they feature results that vastly outweigh their causes, from the perspective of inner truth they offer a perfect balance of cause and effect.

Inner truth is a product of the sense of coldness associated with the early twentieth century, with its two world wars and its modern technological and social revolutions. While some authors, in the process of developing inner truth, focused on the individual (such as in stream-of-consciousness writings), others focused instead on the collective, the race, or a universal psychological experience. When inner truth is transformed into fiction's inner causality, however, inner causality becomes a partial and conditional writing technique. In contrast to zero and partial causality, inner causality cannot truly control a story or generate a great literary perspective that may become a catalyst for a world literary revolution. For this reason, after inner-causal writing was conceived in twentieth-century literature, it offered the literature that came after it a new space and possibility. In fiction, the way inner causality (which is to say, the reality of the soul and the spirit) promotes and transforms objective experience is perhaps precisely the new literary mode that is currently emerging in contemporary Chinese literature—namely, mythorealism.

3   THE POSSIBILITY OF INNER REALITY

If we run into difficulties in our search for canonical works that could have the same significance for inner causality as Kafka's works had for zero causality, or that García Márquez's works had for partial causality, or that Tolstoy's, Dostoevsky's, Balzac's, and Flaubert's works had for full causality—those difficulties could perhaps be seen as a new space that God has given literature's existence and development. In Heller's work, for instance, we find a fresh, distinctive inner truth, but in the end, this truth simply follows in Yossarian's footsteps, heading toward either partial and full causality. In Woolf's works, meanwhile, we find an inner truth that, although more disjointed and fragmented, is also more specific. However, the truth in Woolf's works represents a move toward a causality that dissolves and resists existing causal logics and even attempts to separate itself from them, as one might attempt to flee from a conflagration; on the other hand, when fiction is truly unable to separate itself from stories, it has no choice but to contort itself in order to approach and accommodate full causality.

In the end, the inner-causal logic in these works is like a string of bubbles on a lake's surface—they seem to appear out of nowhere and quickly disappear back into an existing causality. Inner-causal novels rely on inner reality to propel their plot and fictional characters, which is something that we can't find in canonical literary works. These sorts of great works are perhaps a neurotic fantasy developed by someone who loves literature—like a mental patient who, on a rainy day, has a golden sun suddenly sprout from his head, and although this sun might appear enormous and bright, it still wouldn't be real. Or perhaps these sorts of works already exist, but due to our ignorance we therefore lose the opportunity to read them—the same way that we might miss a date with a potential lover. Or, perhaps works with this sort of completely new aesthetic significance are hidden in a corner of one of world's languages, and those authors whose mission it is to use many languages are already the object of an elaborate game of hide-and-seek.

For instance, over a decade ago I stumbled across a story titled "The Third Bank of the River" by a Brazilian author whose name I can never remember, and ever since I haven't been able to get the story out of my mind. I feel like someone who, trapped on a deserted island, hears a faint rescue sound coming from far away—and while on the one hand I may suspect that this is merely a natural sound and not a boat that could come to my rescue, on the other hand, in my desperation I find myself unable to forget that distant and indistinct sound. Every time I think of inner causality—which my fellow writers might view as merely empty words—this story invariably surges forth from my memory:

THE THIRD BANK OF THE RIVER

My father was a dutiful, orderly, straightforward man. And according to several reliable people of whom I inquired, he had had these qualities since adolescence or even childhood. By my own recollection, he was neither jollier nor more melancholy than the other men we knew. Maybe a little quieter. It was Mother, not Father, who ruled the house. She scolded us daily—my sister, my brother, and me. But it happened one day that Father ordered a boat.

He was very serious about it. It was to be made specially for him, of mimosa wood. It was to be sturdy enough to last twenty or thirty years and just large enough for one person. Mother carried on plenty about it. Was her husband going to become a fisherman all of a sudden? Or a hunter? Father said nothing. Our house was less than a mile from the river, which around there was deep, quiet, and so wide you couldn't see across it.

I can never forget the day the rowboat was delivered. Father showed no joy or other emotions. He just put on his hat as he always did and said good-by to us. He took along no food or bundle of any sort. We expected Mother to rant and rave, but she didn't. She looked very pale and bit her lip, but all she said was "If you go away, stay away. Don't ever come back!"

Father made no reply. He looked gently at me and motioned me to walk along with him. I feared Mother's wrath, yet eagerly obeyed. We headed toward the river together. I felt bold and exhilarated, so much so that I said, "Father, will you take me with you in your boat?"

He just looked at me, gave me his blessing, and by a gesture, told me to go back. I made as if to do so but, when his back was turned, I ducked behind some bushes to watch him. Father got into the boat and rowed away. Its shadow slid across the water like a crocodile, long and quiet.

Father did not come back. Nor did he go anywhere, really. He just rowed and floated across and around, out there in the river. Everyone was appalled. What had never happened, what could not possibly happen, was happening. Our relatives, neighbors, and friends came over to discuss the phenomenon.

Mother was ashamed. She said little and conducted herself with great composure. As a consequence, almost everyone thought (though no one said it) that Father had gone insane. A few, however, suggested that Father might be fulfilling a promise he had made to God or to a saint, or that he might have some horrible disease, maybe leprosy, and that he left for the sake of the family, at the same time wishing to remain fairly near them.

Travelers along the river and people living near the bank on one side or the other reported that Father never put foot on land, by day or night. He just moved about on the river, solitary, aimless, like a derelict. Mother and out relatives agreed that the food which he had doubtless hidden in the boat would soon give out and that then he would either leave the river and travel off somewhere (which would be at least more respectable) or he would repent and return home.

How far from the truth they were! Father had a secret source of provisions: me. Every day I stole food and brought it to him. The first night after he left, we all lit fires on the shore and prayed and called to him. I was deeply distressed and felt a need to do something more. The following day I went down to the river with a load of corn bread, a bunch of bananas, and some bricks of raw brown sugar. I waited impatiently a long, long hour. Then I saw the boat, far off, alone, gliding almost imperceptibly on the smoothness of the river. Father was sitting in the bottom of the boat. He saw me but he did not row toward me or make any gesture. I showed him the food and then I placed it in a hollow rock on the river bank; it was safe there from animals, rain, and dew. I did this day after day, on and on and on. Later I learned to my surprise that Mother knew what I was doing and left food around where I could easily steal it. She had a lot of feelings she didn't show.

Mother sent for her brother to come and help on the farm and in business matters. She had the schoolteacher come and tutor us children at home because of the time we had lost. One day, at her request, the priest put on his vestments, went down to the shore, and tried to exorcise the devils that had got into my father. He shouted that father had a duty to cease his unholy obstinacy. Another day she arranged to have two soldiers come and try to frighten him. All to no avail. My father went by in the distance, sometimes so far away he could barely be seen. He never replied to anyone and no one ever got close to him. When some newspapermen came in a launch to take his picture, Father headed his boat to the other side of the river and into the marshes, which he knew like the palm of his hand but in which other people quickly got lost. There in his private maze, which extended for miles, with heavy foliage overhead and rushes on all sides, he was safe.

We had to get accustomed to the idea of Father's being out on the river. We had to but we couldn't. We never could. I think I was the only one who understood to some degree what our father wanted and what he did not want. The thing I could not understand at all was how he stood the hardship. Day and night, in sun and rain, in heat and in the terrible midyear cold spells, with his old hat on his head and very little clothing, week after week, month after month, year after year, unheedful of the waste and emptiness in which his life was slipping by. He never set foot on earth or grass, on isle or mainland shore. No doubt he sometimes tied up the boat at a secret place, perhaps at the tip of some island, to get a little sleep. He never lit a fire or even struck a match and he had no flashlight. He took only a small part of the food that I left in the hollow rock—not enough, it seemed to me, for survival. What could his state of health have been? How about the continual drain on his energy, pulling and pushing the oars to control the boat? And how did he survive the annual floods, when the river rose and swept along with it all sorts of dangerous objects—branches of trees, dead bodies of animals—that might suddenly crash against his little boat?

He never talked to a living soul. And we never talked about him. We just thought. No, we could never put our father out of mind. If for a short time we seemed to, it was just a lull from which we would be sharply awakened by the realization of his frightening situation.

My sister got married, but Mother didn't want a wedding party. It would have been a sad affair, for we thought of him every time we ate some especially tasty food. Just as we thought of him in our cozy beds on a cold, stormy night—out there, alone and unprotected, trying to bail out the boat with only his hand and a gourd. Now and then someone would say that I was getting to look more and more like my father. But I knew that by then his hair and beard must have been shaggy and his nails long. I pictured him thin and sickly, black with hair and sunburn, and almost naked despite the articles of clothing I occasionally left for him.

He didn't seem to care about us at all. But I felt affection and respect for him, and, whenever they praised me because I had done something good, I said, "My father taught me to act that way."

It wasn't exactly accurate but it was a truthful sort of lie. As I said, Father didn't seem to care about us. But then why did he stay around there? Why didn't he go up the river or down the river, beyond the possibility of seeing us or being seen by us? He alone knew the answer.

My sister had a baby boy. She insisted on showing Father his grandson. One beautiful day we all went down to the riverbank, my sister in her white wedding dress, and she lifted the baby high. Her husband held a parasol above them. We shouted to Father and waited. He did not appear. My sister cried; we all cried in each other's arms.

My sister and her husband moved far away. My brother went to live in a city. Times changed, with their usual imperceptible rapidity. Mother finally moved too; she was old and went to live with her daughter. I remained behind, a leftover. I could never think of marrying. I just stayed there with the impediments of my life. Father, wandering alone and forlorn on the river, needed me. I knew he needed me, although he never even told me why he was doing it. When I put the question to people bluntly and insistently, all they told me was that they heard that Father had explained it to the man who made the boat. But now this man was dead and nobody knew or remembered anything. There was just some foolish talk, when the rains were especially severe and persistent, that my father was wise like Noah and had the boat built in anticipation of a new flood. I dimly remember people saying this. In any case, I would not condemn my father for what he was doing. My hair was beginning to turn gray.

I have only sad things to say. What bad had I done, what was my great guilt? My father always away and his absence always with me. And the river always with me. And the river, always the river, perpetually renewing itself. The river, always. I was beginning to suffer from old age, in which life is just a sort of lingering. I had attacks of illness and anxiety. I had a nagging rheumatism. And he? Why, why was he doing it? He must have been suffering terribly. He was so old. One day, in his failing strength, he might let the boat capsize; or he might let the current carry it downstream, on and on, until it plunged over the waterfall to the boiling turmoil below. It pressed upon my heart. He was out there and I was forever robbed of my peace. I am guilty of I know not what, and my pain is an open wound inside me. Perhaps I would know—if things were different. I began to guess what was wrong.

Out with it! Had I gone crazy? No, in our house that word was never spoken, never through all the years. No one called anybody crazy, for nobody is crazy. Or maybe everybody. All I did was go there and wave a handkerchief so he would be more likely to see me. I was in complete command of myself. I waited. Finally he appeared in the distance, there, then over there, a vague shape sitting in the back of the boat. I called to him several times. And I said what I was so eager to say, to state formally and under oath. I said it as loud as I could:

"Father, you have been out there long enough. You are old.... Come back, you don't have to do it anymore.... Come back and I'll go instead. Right now, if you want. Any time. I'll get into the boat. I'll take your place."

And when I had said this, my heart beat more firmly.

He heard me. He stood up. He maneuvered with his oars and headed the boat toward me. He had accepted my offer. And suddenly I trembled, deep down. For he had raised his arm and waved—the first time in so many, so many years. And I couldn't.... In terror, my hair on end, I ran. I fled madly. For he seemed to come from another world. And I'm begging forgiveness, begging, begging.

I experienced the dreadful sense of cold that comes from deadly fear, and I became ill. Nobody ever saw or heard from him again. Am I a man, after such a failure? I am what never should have been. I am what must be silent. I know it is too late. I must stay in the deserts and unmarked plains of my life, and I fear I shall shorten it. But when death comes I want them to take me and put me in a little boat in this perpetual water between the long shores; and I, down the river, lost in the river, inside the river ... the river.[3]

In quoting almost plagiaristically this entire short story here, I am surely violating all standard rules and practices for literary commentary. However, by reading this story in its entirety, we can effectively pinpoint inner-causal discourse. Although "The Third Bank of the River" is not, strictly speaking, an example of inner-causal writing, the story nevertheless offers the following insights about inner causality:

1   Inner causality's inner truth is the engine that drives a story's development, and it controls a story's direction the way a flight plan controls an airplane's trajectory. In this particular story the father purchases a boat and one day gets into the boat and leaves home. For the next several decades, he never returns to shore and instead continually rows back and forth in the middle of the river. In this tear-jerking narrative, the simplest element of inner reality is the conflict between a sense of responsibility and a desire to escape, which will probably be familiar to anyone who has been married and had children. Readers who have had this sort of experience would not doubt this story's underlying truth. This demonstrates that as long as inner-truth writing manages to find an inner truth (which is to say, inner spirit) that doesn't exist in real life but which exists within people's soul or spirit, it will thereby find the rational logic of inner causality. Meanwhile, the question of the novel's realism no longer needs to be considered.

2   Inner-causal works inevitably have an allegorical or mysterious quality, similar to what we find in "The Third Bank of the River," yet they are definitely not allegorical works in their own right. Instead, this allegorical quality derives from the fact that inner truth is something that can only be experienced and expressed by the author, while readers will have never experienced it in real life—the same way that classical allegories could only emerge from a process of circulation and rarely were re-occurrences of actual events. However, the objective of inner-causal writings is not allegory and mystery, nor is it the emotion and allegorical significance contained in the story, but rather it is an attempt to find another way to access reality and vital truth. Inner-causal writings use an innovative approach to write a kind of new reality and truth, which is the fundamental possibility of inner causality, and otherwise inner causality would lose its significance and be suffocated by the invisible hand of allegory and mystery.

3   Inner causality can be exaggerated and ironic, as in *Catch-22*, or calm and leisurely, as in *Mrs. Dalloway*, or solemn and wounded, as in "The Third Bank of the River." Inner causality is not merely a style or sensibility but rather a way of understanding the world, as well as a new path into reality. It is an author's literary perspective and worldview, and if it does not become an author's worldview, at least it can be the author's personality and technique. If inner causality does succeed in becoming

an author's worldview, however, literature may thereby come to have a new telescope extending from fiction to reality, with a structure and result that are completely different from what preceded it. This virtual telescope can look past the doubt left behind zero causality and perceive the murky, semibelievable truth of partial causality. This will lead readers to an inner level of reality that was previously obscured by full causality.

The Brazilian author João Guimarães Rosa probably won't be elevated to the ranks of great authors on the basis of his modest oeuvre of works like his collection *The Devil to Pay in the Backlands*, which did not receive much attention when it was released. In "The Third Bank of the River," however, Rosa managed to use a simple yet poetic narrative that was only about three thousand Chinese characters long (in translation) to communicate an experience of emotional conflict that has universal resonances. As a result, an utterly impossible story allowed us to experience a fundamentally true shared emotion. This, in turn, permitted inner causality—within a space of absolute impossibility—to achieve something that is completely true, and thereby grant us a path of inner-casual writing that follows a trajectory from impossible to possible to completely real, whereby fiction offers more paths by which to achieve truth.

The true bank in "The Third Bank of the River" is a desire to escape the bonds of marriage and family, together with their inevitable emotional conflicts. Just as the story's "third bank" cannot separate itself from full causality or full-causal narration, similarly inner-causal fiction is ultimately unable to leave behind the support offered by full, partial, and zero causality. In the absence of any other available causality, inner causality is truly a form of literary "empty speech"—the same way that the last emperor might, in an attempt to demonstrate his authority, issue a meaningless directive to the officials and commoners who have already betrayed him. However, inner causality's autonomy and independence will ultimately be determined by whether it manages to reject full, partial, and zero causality, because otherwise it will remain enclosed by them and will ultimately fall into the trap of allegory and absurdity, mystery and magic—like someone who, because of his short stature, is liable to be overlooked in a crowd. In the end, inner causality needs to use inner truth to control causality and reality, rather than having reality control causality, or having other causalities control inner causality. Under causality's classifications and rules, works like *The Metamorphosis*, *The Castle*, and *One Hundred Years of Solitude* are all bona fide masterpieces—and they demonstrate that within inner-causal writing, inner truth is inner causality's imperial seal, its talisman, and the basis of its dominance. Meanwhile, inner causality's authority over other forms of causality is like the relationship between a rook and a pawn in chess, or between the main road and side road of a new thoroughfare.

4 ADDITIONAL REFLECTIONS ON INNER CAUSALITY

Literary history has repeatedly demonstrated that in a global context, there is no great author who is simultaneously a great critic, just as it is very rare to find a great critic who is also a great author. This is similar to the way that regardless of how extraordinary a pilot might be, he or she won't be able to fly a train, or how no matter how miraculous a driver might be, he won't be able to drive his car through the air. When Jean-Paul Sartre began writing fiction everyone recognized that he was a great, successful, and unique philosopher, and although he was subsequently awarded the Nobel Prize for Literature, we nevertheless still can't say that he is a great novelist. Conversely, when Camus began writing philosophy, it was recognized that his novels had considerable literary significance and aesthetic value, though his achievement as a philosopher simply cannot be compared to Sartre's. Just as philosophy may be deeper and richer than literature but cannot guide the writing process, similarly theory cannot guide an author's fictional composition. Theory can only tell authors that they should try to proceed in a certain direction and where they might find a new literary path, but it cannot tell them that, say, they should head east, and that after going over the mountain they'll be able to pick up the sun.

Just as Defoe, when he wrote *Robinson Crusoe*, had no idea what realism was, because literary critics had not yet introduced this word to the world, when Kafka wrote *The Metamorphosis* he similarly could not have anticipated the subsequent development of expressionism, modernism, and absurdism. Similarly, when García Márquez was writing *One Hundred Years of Solitude*, he knew about marvelous realism but had no idea that he was in the process of completing a work that would come to be regarded as a perfect exemplar of magical realism, and therefore he later claimed that the artistic achievement of *No One Writes to the Colonel* exceeded that of *One Hundred Years of Solitude*. These and countless other examples illustrate the fundamental rule that great critics may understand how great authors write their works, but great authors never know for certain how they managed to produce their own innovative works. An author's best position is perhaps appearing to know and understand, while anxiously searching. Literature's trajectory from inner truth to inner causality to mythorealism might appear to be completely understood—but in fact it is not necessarily a trajectory that authors are really able to traverse, precisely because it is too obvious.

No literary theory is capable of directing an author exactly how to write, and instead authors can only embark on a process of trial and error, paying a huge price for the possibility of an unexpected reward.

All great works of literature are unexpected outcomes of the author's writing process. If authors, before setting pen to paper, already knew that they were about to produce a great work, they would inevitably fall into an elaborate trap. Inner causality is not a compass capable of guiding the writing process but instead merely a sort of murky possibility. It is not a kind of literary imagination but rather an indistinct result—a half-shrouded direction. Even if an author blindly heads in this direction, he or she will not necessarily be able to enter literature's Forbidden City, though he or she may, at least, enter the most absurd and most complex—not to mention the richest and deepest—truth of contemporary China's reality.

For readers a literary work is a kind of aesthetic, for authors it is a kind of fate, and for reality it is a kind of conduit. But based on inner truth's inner causality, if these three modalities do not offer a new possibility, it is because there is a solid wall erected over that road. However, even if an author becomes a laughingstock by walking directly into this wall, the blood flowing from his forehead may eventually scab over and produce a beautiful design like a dried flower.

6 Mythorealism

1 A SIMPLE EXPLANATION OF MYTHOREALISM

I am certainly violating a crucial taboo when I say I believe contemporary Chinese literature already contains a body of writing that diverges from both nineteenth-century realism and twentieth-century modernism. Or, at the very least, we can say that the sprouts of this new writing have already begun to emerge—though due to the laziness of critics who don't have the patience to perform a careful analysis, these sprouts often end up getting overlooked. This overlooked literature is precisely what I am calling *mythorealism*.

In simple terms, it can be said that mythorealism is a creative process that rejects the superficial logical relations that exist in real life to explore a kind of invisible and "nonexistent" truth—a truth that is obscured by truth itself. Mythorealism is distinct from conventional realism, and its relationship to reality is not driven by direct causality but instead involves a person's soul and spirit (which is to say, the connection between a person and the real relationship between spirit and interior objects) and an author's conjectures grounded in a real foundation. Mythorealism is not a bridge offering direct access to truth and reality, and instead it relies on imaginings, allegories, myths, legends, dreamscapes, and magical transformations that grow out of the soil of daily life and social reality.

Mythorealism does not definitely reject reality; it attempts to create reality and surpass realism.

Mythorealism draws on twentieth-century modernism, even as it simultaneously seeks to position itself outside of twentieth-century literature's various "isms" to root itself in the soil of our own national culture. The difference between mythorealism and other modes of writing lies in the fact that mythorealism pursues inner truth and relies on inner causality to reach the interior of people and society—and in this way it attempts to write truth and create truth.

Mythorealism's distinctiveness, accordingly, lies in its ability to create truth.

2 MYTHOREALISM'S CREATION OF REALITY'S SOIL AND CONTRADICTIONS

From the perspective of reality, literature is merely an accessory—with the type of reality determining the type of literature. From the perspective of literature itself, however, reality is the source material, and after life has been transformed into literature, it is no longer life but rather becomes literature. Writing life simply as life would be like a factory that transforms raw materials into precisely the same raw materials. It would be like taking firewood from a field and arranging it into neat piles a warehouse—but in the end, these new piles of firewood would still just be firewood. When firewood is ignited inside an author's heart, however, its energy may be converted into a new extraordinary object: literature. Life is comparable to those piles of firewood—and while some people may see in life the seasons, years, and the passing of time, others may see household affairs and the troubles of life, others may see poetry and the universe, while others may see only disorder and boredom. The reality of contemporary China has reached the point where it does not consist simply of piles of firewood, crops, or building tiles, but rather it possesses unprecedented complexity, absurdity, and richness.

From the perspective of literature, contemporary China's reality is a vast mud hole containing both gold and mercury, and while some authors may discover glittering gold in the mud hole, others will find that the liquid emerging from their pens is but toxic mercury. We could use the saying *public morality is not what it used to be* to describe contemporary China and its people, because it is impossible to understand the real circumstances of people today. Phrases like *moral degeneracy*, *confused values,* and *having reached the baseline for being human* are all lamentations about contemporary guidelines for society and people, and they simply demonstrate literature's inability to control society and the precarity of our own outmoded attitudes toward literature. These phrases don't, however, offer a fresher and deeper understanding of society and its people. Everyone knows that contemporary China's richness, complexity, strangeness, and absurdity vastly exceed that of its contemporary literature, and while everyone complains that we don't have any great authors and literary works that could do justice to our contemporary era, this ignores the fact that for a long time our literature has sought merely to describe reality rather than to actively explore it. In contemporary literature realism is understood to be a sketch of life, and it is assumed that an author's talent lies simply in selecting appropriate pigments for those sketches. Works that describe reality are celebrated, while those that attempt to explore it are criticized. Because our realism sees its role as simply to describe reality, praise people and society, and exalt beauty and warmth, we therefore rarely find works that dare to truly to question people and society. We lament the fact that we don't have works like Tolstoy's that describe great social transformations, even as we lionize those works that simply describe social reality. Similarly, we complain that we don't have works like Dostoevsky's that interrogate the soul, even as we sing the praises of works that have absolutely nothing to do with the human soul.

When contemporary authors approach the deep truth of people's relationship to China, they must confront three realities. First, they must confront how, in our realist writing, constructed truth is separate from—but simultaneously controls—deep truth. Second, they must confront how worldly-truth classics use a combination of temptation and persuasion to approach vital and spiritual-depth truth. In contrast to constructed truth's efforts to actively undermine authors' will to write, this latter approach is gentler but also more pernicious, because it is more capable of taking away the ideals and ideas with which authors seek deep truth. Third, they must confront the unique reality and writing environment of our simultaneously open and closed society.

In our contemporary writing environment every author must confront a combination of post-Reform monetary temptations, entrapments of privilege, and ideological constraints, thereby helping ensure that contemporary Chinese literature will be unable—or at least unwilling—to proceed in the direction of realist deep truth. These new ideological constraints are not simply a product of the Reform and Opening Up campaign. On the path to the vital truth, these constraints far exceed constructed truth's attitudes of being "not permitted," "not able," and "not allowed," and instead they are a result of the combined influence of politics and finance on contemporary authors' instinctive and unconscious sense of being "not willing." These new constraints make contemporary authors willing to abandon their pursuit of some kind of truth, as a result of which they don't aspire to the innermost level of social reality or humanity's inner heart. Over time, authors will find that their inner heart—whether they acknowledge it or not—develops a barrier between their self and deep reality, and they will instinctively cultivate a habit of self-regulation and self-censorship when they write. There is the rich and complex social reality and the world of the human heart, but there are also barriers preventing authors from attaining this rich and complex society, together with instinctive constraints on the authors' own writing. I believe that all authors inevitably write under these constraints, and that they understand that in contemporary literature's process of literary composition, modernism's attempts to describe reality cannot attain the depth or breadth of realism for which they yearn. Realism stops at a partial understanding of the world and is unable to uncover realities featuring more absurd and bizarre elements, even as authors' struggles to break through these constraints have already become contemporary literature's greatest source of anxiety and exhaustion.

For instance, Yu Hua has observed that in writing *Brothers* he was describing our country's pain, which demonstrates his understanding of and dissatisfaction with contemporary realist literary composition, together with his embrace of "new realism." However, in their response to this novel, many readers and critics remained grounded in an older realism, as evidenced in the way that portions of the novel that exceed the truth and logic of real life became the primary objects of readers' contempt, controversy, and mockery. For instance, the "toilet-peeping" description in Part I of the novel and the "hymen competition" sequence in Part II made almost all readers and critics laugh uproariously and spit in contempt. If we were to summarize the critics' assessment in one word, it would be "dirty," though if we were to assess other literary works by a similar metric, we would have to concede that classics like *On the Road*, *Tropic of Cancer*, *Lolita*, *Lady Chatterley's Lover*, and *Gravity's Rainbow* are not particularly clean either.

The root of the controversy over Yu Hua's *Brothers* is not an aesthetic question of whether the work is clean or dirty but rather the fact that some of the novel's plotlines exceed many readers' understanding of realist writing. The novel itself does not truly attempt to surpass realism. If we look to the work for some kind of truth corresponding to real life, we discover that the toilet-peeping and hymen competition sections surpass a certain truth and logic that people associate with real life, and therefore it is perhaps not surprising that the work was the object of considerable controversy and critique. Similarly, the self-castration scene in Jia Pingwa's *Qin Opera* and the floating heads scene in Su Tong's *The Boat to Redemption* make readers feel as though grains of "suprarealist" or "nonrealist" sand had gotten embedded in their realist eyes. However, if we read these sections from a different perspective—which is to say, if we observe realist literature through the lens of mythorealism—these sections that surpass the old rules of realism instead come to acquire a certain kind of "mythorealist" significance, making them a prototype of mythorealism. Today, real life is replete with pornographic culture and erotic reality, and while the hymen competition scene in *Brothers* might not necessarily be the best literary performance, it does offer a good mythorealistic reflection on reality, thereby rendering the scene an attempt to pursue mythorealism within the context of a realist novel. The hymen competition surpasses conventional reality and approaches "mythoreality"—thereby attaining a truth that is obscured by truth, but which nevertheless contains a conjectural and invisible truth. If we approach these controversial plots from the perspective of mythorealism, accordingly, we discover that the floating heads, toilet-peeping, self-castration, and hymen competition scenes enrich these otherwise realistic works, marking a path toward the complex and absurdist new realism to which contemporary Chinese literary realism aspires.

The key question, however, is whether the act of introducing mythorealist elements into realist works is like mixing water with milk, or like mixing water with oil. Why is it that when this mythorealist "new truth" is introduced into a realist work, it is invariably accompanied by a strong sensory stimulation and physiological response? This is probably a trap into which contemporary literature is liable to fall when a work's mythorealist elements exceed the rules of realism. For instance, García Márquez describes how, in *One Hundred Years of Solitude*, whenever Aureliano Segundo has sex with his mistress, Petra Cotes, all the animals on his farm would suddenly become remarkably fecund. In this semi-causal novel, this scene functions as a kind of miraculous reality, but if a similar scene had appeared in a fundamentally realist work it would have been criticized as an obtrusive and gimmicky oddity. Meanwhile, *Brothers* is not, strictly speaking, a mythorealist work. Yu Hua himself is more inclined to view it as a realist novel, and it is true that the work belongs to a version of realism. However, I cite the novel here simply to illustrate how, when an author attempts to master the unprecedented absurdist reality of contemporary China, he will sense the contradictions between the relatively closed nature of contemporary realism and the almost unlimited openness of real life. This kind of contradiction between reality and literary creation makes an author feel confused, exhausted, and unable to proceed.

For the past three decades, contemporary Chinese literature's repeated attempts to borrow techniques and characteristics from various different branches of Western literary modernism demonstrate that sometimes Western literary trends and local Chinese experiences don't necessarily accord with one another. This, in turn, makes us realize that the birth of any new literary trend cannot escape the reality and the nativist cultural soil of the corresponding era. Perhaps the emergence of mythorealism in contemporary Chinese literature was spawned precisely by the contradictions that exist between the unprecedented richness, complexity, and absurdity of contemporary Chinese reality and the long-standing conventions of realism.

3 THE CONTEMPORARY CREATION OF MYTHOREALIST NOVELS

Here, it is worth recalling two stories from the early eighties: Shen Rong's "Reduced by Ten Years" and Wu Ruozeng's "The Jadeite Cigarette Holder." The former describes how, after everyone loses a full decade of their lives during the Cultural Revolution, the government issues a mandate specifying that everyone who lived through the period can have ten years deducted from their official age. This way, those who are at retirement age won't immediately need to retire, and those who are in danger of missing out on a promotion because they are too old can instead became young cadres who must be quickly promoted. Meanwhile, the latter work describes an old peasant who is filled with optimism because he owns a precious jadeite cigarette holder, and all the other villagers are proud that someone in their community owns such a valuable artifact. Eventually an antiques expert from the city comes to the village, and he immediately recognizes that the jadeite is fake. However, not only does this expert not disclose the truth, he even tells all the villagers that the implement is priceless, but asks them not to show it to anyone else. Therefore, this fake jadeite becomes a spiritual support of lives of the peasant and the other villagers, even if they don't ever show it to anyone else.

These two stories were quite influential when they were initially published, and "Reduced by Ten Years" even won a national literary prize. In the end, however, when compared with mainstream works—like Shen Rong's own *At Middle Age*—these two stories were like small streams in the shadow a mighty river, and over time they were nearly forgotten. The reason I bring them up here is because they are the first works from the Reform era to clearly contain mythorealist elements. This is particularly true of "Reduced by Ten Years," which describes how a "groundless" central government document dictated that ten years be deducted from the age of everyone who had survived the Cultural Revolution. This is an impossible truth, a nonexistent truth, a truth obscured by truth. It is a mythorealist truth obscured by realist truth. Within fiction, this kind of inner truth controls fiction's new causal relation—namely, inner causality. Unfortunately, not long after these two stories were published, Chinese literature fractured into a variety of different trends and movements. Root-seeking literature, for instance, was full of folk culture flavor, and although you'd be hard-pressed to find any mythorealist elements at all in a work like Wang Anyi's novel *Baotown*, its ambiance was full of the sort of mysterious, folk, and sorcery elements that we find in many mythorealist works. Similarly, Han Shaogong's *Bababa*, Jia Pingwa's *The Auspicious Gravesite*, and Li Rui's Deep Earth series all contain mythorealist descriptions or plotlines, though the subjects of these works are fundamentally realist, and the works' stories and characters only occasionally feature some plot or subplots that exceed full causality, having a murky semi-causal and inner-causal existence, which give readers a mythorealist flavor like a barely perceptible breeze. The "new discovery" fiction spearheaded by Su Tong, Yu Hua, and Ge Fei, meanwhile, clearly drew on the experience of twentieth-century Western literature to resist the long-standing perception, in China, that literature should be put into the service of politics. At the same time, this also permitted the murky, hazy, and unconscious mythorealism to have a new source of extraction. This period's new-discovery fiction opened a new window to world literature for post-Reform Chinese literature, and in the process it inadvertently gave subsequent mythorealist literary works a modernist literary preparation.

With *Red Sorghum*, Mo Yan gave Chinese literature a desire to take off, though it was his story "Transparent Carrot," which received much less attention at the time, that ended up making a greater impression on later readers. If we examine Mo Yan's works from the perspective of mythorealism, however, his novel *Republic of Wine* has an even more extraordinary significance. The many transformations that Mo Yan's writing has undergone, combined with his unbridled style of writing, have effectively united traditional Chinese writing and modern Western writing. Although many critics have studied Mo Yan's work, they have not yet succeeded in tracing its literary origins. In their reading of Mo Yan, most critics take as their starting point Latin America's magical realism, while Mo Yan himself tends to emphasize his relationship with Faulkner. However, if we approach Mo Yan's work from the perspective of mythorealism, it is possible to organize his vast, complex oeuvre around a clearer concept, thereby allowing the portions of his novels that surpass realism to acquire a clearer structure and a content that is easier to understand and more replete with local Chinese significance.

Because of the structural and narrative complexity of *Republic of Wine*, Mo Yan's talented use of language was relatively constrained in this work, which is also part of the reason why some readers and critics do not fully understand or accept the novel. We naturally cannot ignore the work's structure, but its value from the perspective of mythorealism is even more significant. The story revolves around the infamous "braised baby" incident, though contemporary readers tend to view this incident as an example of exaggeration, the carnivalesque, imagination, and magic. What these readers ignore is precisely the way in which the novel clearly takes our literature's "mythos" tradition and transforms it into a mythoreality that readers do not truly accept. Later, the opening thirty thousand characters or so of Mo Yan's novel *Big Breasts and Wide Hips* describe how the process of "birthing humans" is undervalued compared to the process of "birthing donkeys"—this is also precisely an example of the sort of "spirit that is obscured in life" that is the object of mythorealist writing, and not the truth of a certain logical relationship between life and reality. However, what we are calling "life's spirit" is but another side of sunlight—a dark valley that people have difficulty seeing when they close their eyes at night. The part of *The Sandalwood Death* that was most criticized is the novel's description of dismemberment; however this sort of dismemberment, like the "braised baby" description in *Republic of Wine*, reflects a move from mythos to the mythoreal. If we view Mo Yan's novels through the lens of mythorealism, *Life and Death Are Wearing Me Out* becomes even more significant. Drawing on China's traditional belief in reincarnation, the novel's protagonist is granted the behavior and fate of various animals, such a pig and a dog. From a realist perspective this plotline is merely the story's outer clothing, but if we approach the novel from the perspective of mythorealism, this theme of reincarnation becomes the organizing principle of the novel's content. It represents mythorealism's enrichment of realism, and also marks an important step in realism's approach to mythorealism.

Similarly, Han Shaogong's *A Dictionary of Maqiao*, Zhang Wei's *Old Boat* and *September Allegory*, Chen Zhongshi's *White Deer Plain*, and Li Rui's *Trees without Wind* and *Cloudless Sky* all contain mythorealistic characteristics, even if they are not strictly speaking mythorealist works in their own right.

With respect to contemporary mythorealist writings, what should be emphasized is not how authors deploy a mythos, including magical, mythical, and mysterious elements, but rather how they cross the bridge of mythos to reach the other shore of the "real"—namely, the "new reality" and new truth that are the reality and truth that contemporary realism cannot reach. Like an array of searchlights, mythorealism is able to illuminate all the shadowy spaces that realism cannot reach and is able to render all obscured absurdity and existence perfectly visible, understandable, and perceptible. The challenge with which mythorealism has presented us is whether we'll ever be able to truly abandon some of the attitudes and constraints associated with realism when we write. Will we be able to face the limits of realist description head-on and look beneath the surface level of the world to find that obscured and imperceptible inner world? Will we be able to catch mythorealism's ferry, thereby discovering the hidden countercurrents that lie beneath the reason that rivers must flow east, while at the same time discovering that sort of invisible absurd truth and existence that lies behind the surface causal logic of everyday life that is often not recognized by readers, reason, or causal logic?

Wang Anyi's novel *I Love Bill* contains an unforgettable plotline centered around a group of female criminals who are in prison. Spring's arrival has made the vegetation turn green, flowers bloom, and plants awaken from their winter slumber, but it has also made the female criminals become strangely irritable and passionate, as they begin to mock and curse each other's personalities and bodies. This "spring and feminine mystique" subplot is the novella's divine inspiration, and it contains a kind of inner truth and causality. This kind of inner truth and causality is precisely the most fundamental difference between mythorealist works and other fictional works. This is the author's mythorealist writing, and it immediately permits readers to catch the mythorealist ferry, thereby entering an inner logic that under normal circumstances we would be unable to perceive. Similarly, we may consider the startling opening of Jia Pingwa's *Ruined City*, which describes how the protagonist Zhuang Zhidie lies down beneath a cow and proceeds to drink milk directly from its udder, which is the novel's the clearest expression of mythorealism. This passage earns my sincere admiration, and my only regret is that in *Ruined City* this sort of mythorealist description is too isolated, which is precisely why it strikes many readers as so abrupt. When a mythoreal soul shines through the realist writing of some of Chi Zijian's works, such as her story "Reverse Spirit," it similarly makes readers sigh in appreciation.

With respect to mythorealism in contemporary literature, Yang Zhengguang's story "How Old Dan Became a Tree" resembles João Guimarães Rosa's "The Third Bank of the River," but it has an even greater power of inner truth and inner causality. In Yang Zhengguang's story, Old Dan is a peasant who moves to a new village to flee adversity. However, he is also someone who, wherever he goes, always needs to find an opponent and enemy, because otherwise he'll feel anxious. Therefore, in his new environment, Old Dan constantly searches for someone to be his enemy. The story follows the logical development of the protagonist's unconscious inner truth, until he finally kills his enemy, who had not committed any crime. This story's inner truth and psychological logic belongs not only to Old Dan but also to society, the nation, and humanity. It reminds us of the zero causality of Kafka's *The Trial*, though the causal logic in "How Old Dan Became a Tree" is more dependable than that of *The Trial* and gives readers a sense that the story's fictional scenario could actually occur. This is also the key difference between inner and zero causality. However, like many other contemporary literary works that contain mythorealistic elements, in the end, "How Old Dan Became a Tree" is swallowed up by realism and full causality. Therefore, this fleeting lotus-like appearance of mythorealism cannot avoid being reabsorbed by the vast lake of realism. As a result, readers can perceive only how the writing styles of some authors differ from others, and they don't see the possibility of mythorealism. Although it is often unrecognized, mythrealism exists in contemporary literature.

4   THE EXISTENCE OF A MYTHOREALIST TRADITION

We need not worry about whether mythorealist writing has only just begun to appear in contemporary literature or instead has already taken shape while being overlooked by readers and critics. Instead, what I want to emphasize here is that mythorealism is not something that any one author created from scratch, but rather it is something that Chinese literature has possessed all along. The only thing is that up to now we have not yet examined or researched relevant issues from the perspective of mythorealism. For instance, when Pigsy, in *Journey to the West*, runs amok in Old Gao Village and yearns for a mortal existence—how is this not an example of mythorealist writing? When the novel's four disciples go to the Western Regions to retrieve the sutras and on the way encounter eighty-one tribulations, including demons trying to consume Tripitaka's flesh to become immortal—how can this not be seen as mythorealism functioning as a displacement of humanity's fear of death? We often place Pu Songling's *Strange Tales from the Liao Zhai Studio* in the genre of a "tales of the miraculous," though some of the collection's stories—including "Wolf," "Ying Ning," "Judge Lu," "The Cricket," and "Nie Xiaoqian"—are refined examples of mythorealism. In this collection many stories attempt, in a dexterous and penetrating fashion, to excavate the real from the mythos. In the real of society and people's inner hearts, Pu Songling's mythorealism illuminates the dark corners that cannot be perceived in real life. Similarly, the "taking the East Wind" section of *Romance of the Three Kingdoms* and many plot-lines in *Investiture of the Gods* all possess mythorealistic qualities. The only issue is that in these latter examples the mythoreal perhaps leans too much toward the mythos, giving insufficient attention to the real.

Of course, Lu Xun's stories are models that are very difficult for later authors to surpass. *Call to Arms* and *Hesitation* helped establish Lu Xun as a giant of modern literature, though some readers are more admiring of his *Old Stories Retold*. In the preface to the latter collection, however, Lu Xun noted that most of the pieces are "still in the form of hasty sketches, not worthy of the name of 'story' according to the manuals of literature. In some places the narrative is based on passages in old books, elsewhere I give free reign to my imagination. And having less respect for the ancients than for my contemporaries, I have not always been able to avoid facetiousness."[1] Setting aside Lu Xun's humility, we may observe that many of the stories in his collection feature a loose and perhaps somewhat slick language, yet virtually every work also possesses mythorealistic elements. The stories are set in the past, but their significance lies in the present; mythos functions as their bridge, while the real functions as their other bank; the past is their drive, while the present is the locus of their meaning.

Consider the collection's most famous story, "Forging the Swords," which truly captures the brutality of power. When Lu Xun's works describe feudal power, it is often like the scene in *The True Story of Ah Q*, when Ah Q's spirits are elevated after Mr. Zhao's son passes the *xiucai* level of the civil service examinations, thereby leading Ah Q to claim that he also belongs to a family that can boast of having three generations of *xiucai* graduates. Mr. Zhao therefore summons Ah Q to his house and curses him, saying, "How could *you* be named Zhao?—Do you think you are worthy of the name Zhao?"[2] In "Forging the Swords," meanwhile, Lu Xun describes how, as a result of ruthlessness and opposition of feudal power, the decapitated heads of the king and of Mei Jian Chi begin fighting one another while floating in a cauldron full of boiling water:

> The moment the king's head touched the water, Mei Jian Chi's head came up to meet it and savagely bit its ear. The water in the cauldron boiled and bubbled as the two heads engaged upon a fight to the death. After about twenty encounters, the king was wounded in five places, Mei Jian Chi in seven. The crafty king contrived to slip behind his enemy, and in an unguarded moment Mei Jian Chi let himself be caught by the back of his neck, so that he could not turn round. The king fastened his teeth into him and would not let go, like a silkworm burrowing into a mulberry leaf. The boy's cries of pain could be heard outside the cauldron.[3]

If we compare "Forging the Swords" and *The True Story of Ah Q*, it is clear that the language, dialogue, characters, and structure of the former are not as precise as those of the latter. In fact, there are even sections of the former that may strike some readers as quite crude. However, "Forging the Swords" is in no way inferior to *The True Story of Ah Q* when it comes to the work's ability to encourage readers to reflect on an abusive feudal power system. Of course, the literary significance of *The True Story of Ah Q* lies not only in the manner in which it describes how someone faced with feudal power may adopt a strategy of claiming spiritual victories, just as the significance of "Forging the Swords" does not lie merely in how it uses a legendary story to transmit wisdom regarding humanity's struggle with power. However, with respect to this point that both works share, why is it that we are most astonished by "Forging the Swords"? Why does this story possess such a different aesthetic and thought compared to *The True Story of Ah Q?* This is an illustration of the different aesthetics and validation offered by realism and mythorealism. Realist writings, after all, must be grounded in a foundation of the real, while mythorealism can be grounded in a combination of the real and the mythos. What is particularly important is that mythorealism can—and, indeed, must—be grounded in a mythoreal foundation predicated on an equivalence between mythos and the real, or between the real and mythos.

In *Old Stories Retold*, Lu Xun primarily adopts a realist technique to write about heroes and immortals or celestial beings. He takes the greatness of those celestial or legendary elements and transposes them to the human realm to examine and describe humanity. Lu Xun was already using this technique in the first work from the *Old Stories Retold* volume, "Mending Heaven":

> Nüwa woke with a start.
>
> She was frightened out of a dream, yet unable to remember what she had dreamed; conscious only, rather crossly, of something missing as well as of a surfeit of some kind.[4]

It turns out that even Nüwa, the celestial ancestor of humanity, also sleeps and dreams, and sometimes can even become strangely irritable. In "The Flight to the Moon," the celestial fairy Chang'e, like a resentful wife in a peasant household, complains about having to eat the same meal of noodles with crow sauce every day. Laozi is a wise spirit of our people, a peerless philosopher and the antecedent of Confucius, yet in "Leaving the Pass," when Confucius is about to leave after having come to visit him, Laozi finds the need to play petty games. In "Forging the Swords" Mei Jian Chi, to get revenge, "raised his hand to draw the blue sword from his back and with the same movement swung it forward from the nape of the neck, as his head fell on the green moss at his feet."[5] Then this sixteen-year-old, who looks upon death as a return to home, sees the rat that has fallen into the cauldron and hesitates over whether to rescue it or let it drown.

From 1922 to the time *Old Stories Retold* was published in 1935, Lu Xun already anticipated today's mythorealist writing, and with so many excellent works he showed us that all literary "isms"—including mythorealism—are, in the end, for the sake of the real and for humanity, and not for mythos itself. Therefore, when we look back at the literary traditions that led up to contemporary writing, regardless of whether we consider classic legends or supernatural tales, the nutrition they provide mythorealism should not be a question of how legendary or supernatural the stories are, but rather how they proceed from the supernatural to the human, from the strange to the ordinary, and from the fictitious to the real. It is a question of how they can proceed down the path of the mythoreal and attain that kind of absurd truth that cannot be observed with mortal eyes, and the kind of existence that readers assume—because it is so absurd and weird—cannot exist.

In any case, in our contemporary environment, *Journey to the West* cannot help but give readers a feeling of legend for the sake of legend, just as *Strange Tales from the Liao Zhai Studio* cannot help but give readers a feeling of strangeness for the sake of strangeness. Similarly, Lu Xun's *Old Stories Retold* collection cannot easily distance itself from the sense of deviation associated with the alienation of human and reality that pervades the entire old-stories-retold genre. Nevertheless, these great works all demonstrate that today's mythorealism did not emerge out of nowhere and instead has deep roots in Chinese literature. At the same time, these great works also remind us that what today's mythorealist writing absolutely cannot do is pursue the mythoreal simply for the sake of the mythoreal—because the real world and real humanity would thereby become inflected with the sort of alienation that has been discussed here.

5   THE UNIQUENESS OF MYTHOREALISM
IN CONTEMPORARY WRITING

Contemporary mythoreal writing cannot separate itself from the influence of twentieth-century world literature. This is similar to the way that the video games played by today's youth, regardless of how simple they may be, cannot separate themselves from the twentieth-century technology in which they are grounded. As today's world grows increasingly compressed—like a village where a dog barking on one side will wake up someone sleeping on the other—there is no kind of object or culture that can fully separate itself from others and attain an autonomous existence. This principle also applies to literature, and just as mythorealism cannot separate itself from Chinese tradition and create a world out of nothing, it similarly cannot separate itself from world literature's modernist writing and attain a completely autonomous existence.

If we consider some of the most important contemporary Chinese authors, we find that the nourishment they derive from twentieth-century Western modernism is not at all inferior to that which they have absorbed from the Chinese tradition. Twentieth-century literature circulates in the veins of contemporary Chinese authors, while the mythorealism that has not yet been truly recognized by readers or critics cannot be separated from twentieth-century modernist literature. In fact, one could even say that it is precisely the inspiration that Chinese authors have derived from Western modernism and Latin American magic realism over the past three decades that has helped nourish the seeds from which contemporary Chinese mythorealism has begun to sprout. The reason readers, commentators, and consumers are constantly linking Chinese authors and their works with qualities such absurdism, exaggeration, humor, postmodernism, surrealism, new fiction, existentialism, and magic realism is because our contemporary literature does in fact contain an excessive amount of borrowing and even outright imitation. It is like going to a neighbor's house to borrow clothing for one's own wedding, and though you'll have to return the clothing afterward, you may eventually conceive and bear your own children. Mythorealism is like the child that results from this sort of wedding, and it is difficult for mythorealism to separate itself from its external roots, the same way that it would have been difficult to conduct the wedding without borrowing the neighbor's clothing. The primary difference between this figurative wedding and a process of literary appropriation, however, is that while a marriage may require only a year or two, or perhaps three to five years, to yield offspring, the process of literary appropriation may require a decade or two, or perhaps even longer, to yield results.

This is probably how mythorealism came to appear in contemporary literature. The main difference between mythorealism and the mythoreal elements we find in classic works from the Chinese tradition and modernist works from world literature is that mythorealism exists not primarily for the sake of the mythos but rather for the sake of the real and "people." This difference in the works' initial trajectory, meanwhile, will necessarily influence their ultimate destinations. The foundation of mythorealism requires a destination that is located in the real and the human. If we are willing to be somewhat less precise, we could probably say that from the birth of realism to its peak in the nineteenth century, its primary trajectory has been from society to the human. Humans are inherently social, and without society it would be difficult to have literary characters. In the end, social reality was the stage on which people appeared and was also the stage on which authors developed their works. By the twentieth century, however, this stage had gradually begun to disappear, while people—which is to say, individuals—became the heart of literature's dance of thought. In twentieth-century literature the significance of society gradually diminishes, while people become increasingly central to the literature's dance of thought. Society is positioned behind people, just as an environment is created by people and is not their external world. People or individuals become the primary window through which one's surroundings and the real world may be perceived.

In the nineteenth century, society was used to observe people; while in the twentieth century, people were instead used to observe society.

This kind of formulation is not something everyone can accept, because these factors often become mixed up, rendering it difficult to determine which ultimately takes precedence. Generally speaking, however, this inevitably becomes one form of knowledge. Proceeding from this form of knowledge, the objective of mythorealism is not merely to attain a deeper understanding of a complicated and absurd deep reality (of which history is simply one form). Nor is it simply to analyze a more complicated and absurd human existence. Instead, mythorealism, like reality, seeks to view people and the world as a single, indivisible whole. From the perspective of the methods and paths by which this process is implemented, Western modernist writing pushed stories and characters in the direction of zero and partial causality. In twentieth-century literature, zero and partial causality became literature's catalyst, while traditional full-causal logic became a laughingstock and was cast away by literature's new standard-bearers. Full-causal logic is the shackle that authors have finally shed, as zero causality and partial causality lay the foundation for the pinnacles of twentieth-century literature. The former includes works like Kafka's *The Metamorphosis* and *The Castle*, Samuel Beckett's *Waiting for Godot*, and Eugène Ionesco's *The Bald Soprano*, while the latter includes works like García Márquez's *One Hundred Years of Solitude*. We have already discussed zero causality's and partial causality's significance for a story's meaning and for related processes of literary transformation, but given the influence that these traditions have had on contemporary Chinese literature, they will naturally continue to impact the literary production in the twenty-first century.

After mythorealism received an initial catalyst that was distinct from Western modernism, it developed in a different direction and with a different objective. Realizing that twentieth-century literature was constrained by the shackles of world literature, mythorealism shattered the causal bonds that constrained nineteenth-century literature, while at the same time taking inspiration from zero-causal and semi-causal modern literature. In reality, zero and partial causality are both reactions to full causality; they are the rich and creative causalities from which literature is ultimately unable to separate itself. With the emergence of Chinese literature's mythorealism, many contemporary authors finally managed—after more than two decades of reflection and struggle, writing and realization—to find the rifts in the full-, semi-, and zero-causal fetters from which they ultimately managed to free themselves. They managed to find literature's inner causality. By contrast, literature's full causality—like its partial causality and zero causality—is a form of "outer-causal" constraint.

Full causality is positioned at the beginning of zero causality, just as zero causality is positioned at the end of full causality. Partial causality, meanwhile, represents their sublation and mutual reliance. Based on this analysis, we can view these three types of causality as constituting a loop of outer causality, within which there is a loop of inner causality. Alternatively, inner causality could be viewed as the true origin and terminus of this causal strand—representing a new beginning that has a parallel or opposed existence with it.

The cause, pursued by mythorealist writing, behind a story's development and its characters' transformation cannot be separated from the support of full, partial, or even zero causality, and instead it is even more reliant on inner causality for its development. Readers can no longer directly perceive the logic of daily life in these stories, and instead they must intuit the existence of an internal logic; they can no longer directly perceive a story's causality, much less directly experience it, and instead they must participate in a nonspiritual fashion.

Mythorealism's inner causality, accordingly, is a new form of causality that cannot be experienced directly and instead can only be grasped spiritually. The establishment and confirmation of the deep logic of a story's inner causality marks its greatest difference from Western literary movements such as absurdism, postmodernism, surrealism, and magical realism. This is the basis of mythorealism's distinctive identity within Chinese and world literature. Meanwhile the deep logic of inner causality that is emphasized here is the "human soul, life spirit, and the logic that is virtually undetectable in real life" that is positioned at the core of mythorealism and which drives the development and transformation of fictional stories and characters. The causalities with which everyone is familiar—including the zero causality and partial causality that have already been broadly incorporated into literature—have not disappeared, but instead they have been transformed, revised, or pushed back, to make room for inner causality. Inner causality offers us a new understanding of novels like Mo Yan's *Republic of Wine* and *Life and Death are Wearing Me Out*, not to mention those widely critiqued plotlines in Yu Hua's *Brothers*. There are also those odd mythoreal elements that overflow the borders of realism in works such as *A Dictionary of Maqiao, White Deer Plain, September Allegory, Old Boat, Baotown, Trees without Wind*, and Zhang Chengzhi's *A History of the Soul*. In these sorts of works, we can observe a progression toward a new truth.

Within this eclectic scene of contemporary literary production, mythorealism is perhaps still only at an initial stage. However, if we view mythorealism as a gate in fiction's corner courtyard, then once it has been opened a crack, it allows readers to peer through it and see into the distance—which marks the possibility of the deep truth of an open and distinct, complex and absurd new truth and new reality, and dissimilar people and societies.

6 MYTHOREALISM'S RULES AND DIVINATIONS

Although we may not be able to find any canonical models of mythorealist writing among existing works of contemporary literature, this kind of writing has nevertheless already begun to appear, and furthermore it has come to enjoy a broad existence in many authors' works. Unfortunately, this sort of existence is also a kind of conscious or unconscious scattering. Like seeds blown into a wasteland, where they produce flowering plants, these mythorealist elements have a tendency to fend for themselves and a resigned attitude of governing by doing nothing. This is because fiction cannot be like a building, which must first have a design and a blueprint. Instead, fiction's mysteriousness lies in the way that before a work is written, even the author cannot say with certainty what form the work will ultimately take. Even with the development of modern technologies like X-rays and MRIs, it is still impossible to produce an image of an author's thought or imagination. It is foolhardy to attempt to draw up a strict blueprint for a future work or genre, and instead the best kind of environment for development is perhaps a kind of unsupervised recklessness. Works are born because they have to be born, and they perish because they have to perish. The birth of a great novel relies not only on hard work, but more importantly on a combination of the author's understanding and will, as well as on sheer luck. There is a way, accordingly, in which an author's narration is comparable to the plot's simply spilling onto the ground. Mythorealist writing is like seeds that fall on a wasteland, and you cannot water or cultivate these seeds too carefully, but neither can you pretend you didn't see them when they fall on a stone and die.

There is a folk tale titled "A Mother's Heart," and even if it isn't strictly speaking a mythorealist work, we can at least use it to explain some of mythorealism's murky rules.

A MOTHER'S HEART

It is said that, deep in the mountains, a mother lived with her son. The mother and son enjoyed a solitary existence, and relied on each other for survival. However, the son was smart and diligent, and his mother loved him like life itself. Eventually the son reached the age for marriage, and just as his mother was beginning to feel anxious about his prospects, it was announced that the emperor was looking for someone to marry his daughter. The emperor's only condition was that the young man must extract his own mother's heart and transform it into a red diamond for the princess—and only then could he become the emperor's son-in-law.

When the son heard this announcement, he immediately hurried home and told his mother. His mother didn't say a word, and instead continued cooking her son's food and washing his clothes, as usual. Just as the sun was setting, however, the son returned from the mountain, where he had gone to chop firewood. He placed the firewood in a corner of the courtyard, then called out to his mother. When he didn't hear a response from her, he entered the house, and on the table he saw a plate with a bowl over it, to prevent food from getting cold. The son picked up the bowl, and saw that underneath there wasn't food, but rather his mother's still-warm, bloody heart.

The son stared in shock.

From somewhere, the boy heard his mother's voice: "Son, quickly take Mother's heart, and give it to the princess before the sun sets."

Just like that, the boy grasped the warm, soft heart with both hands and rushed toward the princess's palace. He hoped he'd be able to make there before sunset, so that he could give that warm heart to the beautiful, rich, and respected princess. But because he was running too fast down the mountain road, he tripped and fell, whereupon the heart he was holding fell out of his hands and rolled down the mountainside. The boy trembled with shock, afraid that the princess might not want the heart if it was dirty or broken. As though afraid that an actual diamond was rolling away and in danger of breaking or getting lost, he quickly got up and began searching for his mother's heart in stone crevices and among leaves and branches. As he was searching, he heard his mother's heart speaking to him from under a pile of leaves and branches:

"Son, quick, get up. Are you hurt? If you are injured, then on the riverbank up ahead you'll find some water pennywort to stanch the bleeding."

As a result, before sunset the son managed to give his mother's warm heart to the princess. Three days later, he walked out of the forest, and became the emperor's son-in-law.

This legend has the following qualities that either approximate or directly accord with mythorealism:

1   The existence of inner truth—namely, a mother's boundless love for her son, which need not be spoken.

2   Because inner truth appears in the story, it therefore drives the story's inner causality. The reason the mother can still speak after her death is because she has a heart that will love her son forever; and the reason a wet, fleshy heart is able to speak, ask questions, and give the son instructions is also because of the existence of that inner truth.

3   A person's inner truth will determine what kind of result they will have. Inner truth determines the direction of inner causality's mythorealist writings and the result of the story's development. Its distinguishing

characteristics are as follows. First, inner causality does not feature the quality of equivalence that we find in full causality, wherein any cause will necessarily have a commensurate result and the scale of the cause will determine the scale of the result. Second, inner causality is unlike the lack of necessity and logic we find in zero causality—the logical relations in its stories don't necessarily feature a "vital truthfulness." Whereas Gregor Samsa, in *The Metamorphosis*, is transformed into a giant insect for no apparent reason, and K, in *The Castle*, is unable to enter the castle for unspecified reasons, in the case of mythorealism's inner causality, the inner cause rejects reasons that can be lived and experienced. Meanwhile, what mythorealism needs to search for, grasp, or create is an inner cause that is invisible and virtually nonexistent, but which nevertheless must exist in everyone's spirit and soul. Third, whereas partial causality's center of gravity hovers between zero and full causality, what inner causality emphasizes, by contrast, is precisely the possibility of transcending zero and full causality. In the legend discussed, for instance, this is the heart that can speak, can talk about loving and hating the son, and perform other tasks. Inner causality's greatest possibility involves its ability to transcend other causal limits, which is also mythorealism's most distinctive aesthetic appeal.

4   The examples of inner-truth stories cited in this chapter—like "The Third Bank of the River," "A Mother's Heart," and "Forging the Swords"—all use a source of inner truth, from which they develop and narrate a full-causal story. Hidden behind the inner-causal source, is the contribution of zero and partial causality, which make inner causality fall back into myth, allegory, and legend—the same way that we always end up associating Kafka with allegory. As a result, in mythorealist writing there is no single source of causal logic, and instead there are multiple sources—the same way that partial causality has a ubiquitous presence in *One Hundred Years of Solitude*. Is this not grounds for liberating mythorealism from allegory and for letting mythorealism enjoy an autonomous existence, so that it may mature and become embedded in readers' hearts? If—in the narrative behind the multiple sources of inner causality—it were possible to draw zero and partial causality into the story's logic, would not our understanding of mythorealism be clearer and richer?

5   Mythorealism's real dilemma lies not in how we allocate and use inner, partial, zero, and full causality, nor does it imply that we should

place inner causality on a pedestal and relegate all other causalities to an auxiliary position. Instead, the dilemma involves the keen wisdom an author derives from facing real life and the real world. In the end, if you are telling a story and your narrative can't attain the deep truth of humanity, society, and the world, and if it isn't able to enter dark regions that readers and critics can't see, then any narrative method you adopt will necessarily lack any kind of exploratory and aesthetic significance. Because there exists a certain deep truth that cannot be attained and cannot be expressed using conventional means, mythorealism becomes a form of illusory shadowboxing—like a dwarf who appears on stage wearing stilts. In short: mythos is the method and the real is the objective, and mythorealism's precondition lies in its use of mythos in place of the real in exchange for the meaning of deep reality and deep truth, and for fiction's life in readers.

6   When writing truly has a method and direction, its prospects will necessarily lead directly to the author's grave. This is similar to the way viewers who already know the outcome of a ball game will inevitably lose interest in watching it. If every word a fortune-teller uttered were true, everyone's future would be pointless. The reason we want to have our fortunes told is precisely because fortune-telling is often inaccurate, though sometimes it is on the mark. If fortunes were always correct, we would be utterly terrified, and in the end, we wouldn't dare to ask to see them. Mythorealist writings are like a fortune-teller's nagging—and we have never heard a fortune-teller try to predict their own fortune. Perhaps this is because the fortune-teller doesn't really believe in divination, and instead fortune-telling is mere a form of deception that they use to survive. Or perhaps the fortune-teller knows their own future but cannot discuss it, and therefore keeps it close to their heart and doesn't share it with anyone.

There is a Buddhist story that has considerable relevance to our understanding of writing. The story concerns a young monk who was smart, wise, and diligent, but who was unable to attain enlightenment. His fellow monks, after achieving enlightenment, all went to serve as abbots in other temples, and only this one monk remained in his original temple, studying scriptures and meditating. Eventually, one day he asked his master, "Why can't I become a Buddha?" His master replied, "Because you're too smart." The young monk asked, "How can I become more stupid?" His master replied, "Go work the fields." Therefore, the young monk set aside his scriptures and began working in a field next to the temple. Initially, the young monk did not know how to farm. He didn't understand the seasonal nature of farming and didn't know to sow in the spring and harvest in the fall. However, he was diligent and hard-working, and although his yield the first year was poor, by the following year it had significantly improved. By autumn of the third year, the field next to the temple was filled with fruits and vegetables, bright colors and flavorful fragrances. However, when the monk's master came over he looked at this scene, frowned, and was silent for a long time. The young monk asked, "Master, did I not farm well enough?" The master replied, "Yes, you farmed very well. Extremely well." Somewhat discouraged, the young monk asked angrily, "Do you mean that it will only be good if it's not good?" The master replied, "You should continue for another three years." When the master finished speaking, he left uneasily. From that point on, the young monk stopped working cleverly and carefully, and instead he simply sowed the field each spring, weeded after it rained, harvested in the fall, and rested in the winter. When he plowed and sowed in the spring he was rather lazy, but the field remained as fertile as before. After the young monk continued in this way for three more years, one day his master came over from the temple. The master saw that because the field had not yet been harvested many stalks were leaning over, and because the fruit had not been picked, some of it had begun to rot. The master looked around for the young monk, but there was no trace of him in the field. Only after the master reached a distant hermitage did he find the young monk lying in the sun and watching cricket fights. When the young monk saw his master, he was neither happy nor surprised. Instead, he merely bowed, gestured for his master to sit down, then returned to his crickets.

The master said, "Do you know it's harvest time?"

The young monk replied, "Oh, I forgot."

The master said, "Have you learned how to farm?" The young monk replied without hesitation, "I no longer know how." The master monk asked, "How are the crickets doing?" The young monk replied truthfully, "I'm still learning." The master laughed, and said, "You've achieved enlightenment. You are free to leave now." After the young monk departed, he went to chant sutras in another temple and eventually became an eminent monk in his own right.

This is an entertaining story of Buddhist enlightenment, and literature probably also follows a similar principle. Accordingly, mythorealist writing, for me, is not only a sort of Buddhist allegory, but also a kind of divination. For contemporary literature, it is like a fortune-teller who treats what they saw yesterday as a secret text anticipating what will happen tomorrow, and then tells other people. In the time it takes to crack a smile, all solemnity can turn and walk away—like a pilgrim who, after stopping to chat and drink tea, still needs to continue his pilgrimage alone. The pilgrim carries a travel bag, as though waiting for it to become pen and paper.

MING DYNASTY VERNACULAR NOVELS

Investiture of the Gods 封神演義
Journey to the West 西遊記
Plum in the Golden Vase 金瓶梅
Romance of the Three Kingdoms 三國演義

OTHER AUTHORS AND WORKS

Ba Jin 巴金

Cao Xueqin 曹雪芹
    Dream of the Red Chamber 紅樓夢

Chang, Eileen 張愛玲
    "Golden Cangue" 金鎖記
    Love in a Fallen City 傾城之戀
    Red Rose White Rose 紅玫瑰白玫瑰
    "Shutdown" 封鎖

Chen Sihe 陳思和

Chen Zhongshi 陳忠實
    White Deer Plain 白鹿原

Chi Zijian 遲子建
    "Reverse Spirit" 逆行精靈

Feng Menglong 馮夢龍
    Stories from a Ming Collection 三言二拍

Ge Fei 格非

"Ying Ning" 嬰甯

Qian Zhongshu 錢鍾書
  Fortress Besieged 圍城

Shen Congwen 沈從文
  Border Town 邊城
  "The Husband" 丈夫
  The Long River 長河
  "Xiao Xiao" 蕭蕭

Shen Rong 諶容
  At Middle Age 人到中年
  "Reduced by Ten Years" 減去十歲

Su Tong 蘇童
  The Boat to Redemption 河岸

Tao Yuanming 陶淵明
  "Peach Blossom Spring" 桃花源記

Wang Anyi 王安憶
  Baotown 小鮑莊_
  I Love Bill 我愛比爾

Wang Zengqi 汪曾祺
  "Buddhist Initiation" 受戒
  "Chronicles of Danao" 大淖紀事

Wu Ruozeng 吳若增
  "The Jadeite Cigarette Holder" 翡翠煙嘴

Xiao Hong 萧红

Yang Zhengguang 楊爭光
  "How Old Dan Became a Tree" 老旦是棵樹

Yan Lianke 閻連科
  Ballad, Hymn, Ode 風雅頌
  The Day the Sun Died 日熄
  Dream of Ding Village 丁莊夢
  The Explosion Chronicles 炸裂志
  The Four Books 四書
    "A Traitor to Writing" 寫作的叛徒
  Hard Like Water 堅硬如水
  Lenin's Kisses 受活
    "Seeking a Reality Beyond 'Isms'" 尋求超越主義的現實
  The Prison of Emotion 情感獄
  Streams of Time 日光流年
  Three Brothers 我與父輩

The Years, Months, Days 年月日

Yu Dafu 郁達夫

Yue Lin 嶽麟

Yu Hua 余華
  Brothers 兄弟

Zhang Chengzhi 張承志
  A History of the Soul 心靈史

Zhang Wei 張煒
  Old Boat 古船
  September Allegory 九月寓言

Zhou Zuoren 周作人

TRANSLATOR'S INTRODUCTION

1. The journalist Deng Fei 鄧飛 is credited with having helped popularize the term *cancer village* in 2013, when he published a map of several dozen Chinese villages with unusually high cancer rates.
2. Li Tuo 李陀 and Yan Lianke 閻連科, "Shouhuo"《受活》[*Lenin's Kisses*], 208.
3. Yan Lianke, "Xunqiu chaoyuezhuyi de xianshi" 尋求超越主義的現實 [Seeking a reality beyond 'isms'"], 229.
4. Gao Xingjian 高行健, "Mei you zhuyi" 沒有主義 [Without isms], 3–14.
5. Eagleton, *Ideology of the Aesthetic*.
6. Rojas, "Without [Femin]ism."

CHAPTER 1: REALISM'S FOUR LEVELS OF TRUTH

1. Yan Lianke 閻連科, "Xiezuo de pantu" 寫作的叛徒 [A traitor to writing], 229.
2. Jerofejev, "Mourning Soviet Literature," 64; translated from the Chinese.
3. Shen Congwen 沈從文, *Biancheng* 邊城 [Border town], 22.
4. Chen Sihe 陳思和, "Jiliu jinchu ying shi liming" 激流尽处应是黎明 [The end of the torrent should be dawn], 442–43.
5. Coetzee, *Stranger Shores*, 398.
6. Tolstoy, *Anna Karenina*, part 7, chapter 31, 798.
7. Tolstoy, *Anna Karenina*, part 7, chapter 31, 800.
8. Tolstoy, *Anna Karenina*, part 7, chapter 31, 802
9. Coetzee, *Stranger Shores*, 203–4. The embedded reference is to Frank, *Dostoevsky*.
10. Yue Lin 岳麟, preface to the Chinese edition of *Crime and Punishment*, 3.

11. Dostoevsky, *Crime and Punishment*, part 1, chapter 1, 1.
12. Dostoevsky, *Crime and Punishment*, part 2, chapter 2, 93-94.
13. Dostoevsky, *Crime and Punishment*, part 3, chapter 5, 206.
14. Dostoevsky, *Crime and Punishment*, part 5, chapter 4, 329-330.
15. Dostoevsky, *Crime and Punishment*, part 6, chapter 8, 413.
16. Dostoevsky, *The Brothers Karamazov*, book 7, chapter 4, 332-33.
17. Liu Zaifu 劉再復 and Liu Jianmei 劉劍梅, *Gongwu Honglou* 共悟後樓 [Collaboratively understanding Red Chamber], 231.

CHAPTER 2: ZERO CAUSALITY

1. Kafka, "The Metamorphosis," in *The Complete Stories*, 89.
2. Zhou Zuoren 周作人, "Ren de wenxue" 人的文學 [A humane literature]; Wang Zengqi 汪曾琪, *Puqiao ji* 蒲桥集 [Pu Bridge collection], 46.
3. Kafka, "The Metamorphosis," 90.
4. Kafka, "The Metamorphosis," 92, 98.
5. Kafka, "The Metamorphosis," 135–35.
6. Kafka, "The Metamorphosis," 122.
7. Kafka, "The Metamorphosis," 139.
8. Kafka, "The Metamorphosis," 139.
9. Kafka, "Blumfeld, an Elderly Bachelor," in *The Complete Stories*.
10. Kafka, "The Bucket Rider," in *The Complete Stories*, 413.
11. Kafka, "The Hunger Artist," in *The Complete Stories*.
12. Kafka, "The Burrow" and "The Judgement," in *The Complete Stories*, 88.
13. Kafka, "Fragment 15," in *Dearest Father*, 250.
14. Kafka, *The Castle*, 5.
15. Tang Yongkuan 湯永寬, postface to the Chinese edition of *The Castle*, 282.
16. Tang Yongkuan, postface to *The Castle*, 282.

CHAPTER 3: FULL CAUSALITY

1. Tolstoy, *Resurrection*, part 3, chapter 3, 38.

CHAPTER 4: PARTIAL CAUSALITY

1. Kafka, "The Metamorphosis," 89.
2. García Márquez, *One Hundred Years of Solitude*, 8.
3. Tolstoy, *Anna Karenina*, part 1, chapter 1, 13.
4. García Márquez, *One Hundred Years of Solitude*, 68–69.
5. Tolstoy, *Anna Karenina*, part 3, chapter 26, 352.
6. Flaubert, *Madame Bovary*, part 1, chapter 6, 38.
7. Kafka, "The Judgement," in *The Complete Stories*, 87.

8. See "The Nobel Prize in Literature 1982." Accessed August 18, 2021. https://www.nobelprize.org/prizes/literature/1982/summary.
9. García Márquez, *One Hundred Years of Solitude*, 61.
10. García Márquez, *One Hundred Years of Solitude*, 118.
11. Salvidar, *García Márquez*.
12. Mendoza, *The Fragrance of Guava*, 30–31.
13. Mendoza, *The Fragrance of Guava*, 41–42.
14. Mendoza, *The Fragrance of Guava*, 56.
15. Mendoza, *The Fragrance of Guava*, 46.
16. Tolstoy, *Anna Karenina*, part 1, chapter 30, 119.
17. García Márquez, "Eyes of a Blue Dog," in *Collected Stories*, 50–57.
18. García Márquez, "Nabo," in *Collected Stories*, 73–82.
19. García Márquez, "Nabo," 82.
20. Mendoza, *The Fragrance of Guava*, 32.
21. Mendoza, *The Fragrance of Guava*, 124.

CHAPTER 5: INNER CAUSALITY

1. Woolf, *Mrs. Dalloway*, 3.
2. Woolf, "Modern Fiction," 160–61.
3. Rosa, "The Third Bank of the River," 125–30. William Grossman's English translation of the story is reprinted here with permission from University of California Press.

CHAPTER 6: MYTHOREALISM

1. Lu Xun, "The Author's Preface," in *Old Stories Retold*, 3-4.
2. Lu Xun, *The True Story of Ah Q*, 3.
3. Lu Xun, "Forging the Swords," in *Old Stories Retold*, 90.
4. Lu Xun, "Mending Heaven," in *Old Stories Retold*, 5.
5. Lu Xun, "Forging the Swords," in *Old Stories Retold*, 84.

Bibliography

Chen Sihe 陳思和. "Jiliu jinchu ying shi liming" 激流尽处应是黎明 [The end of the torrent should be dawn]. In *Ba Jin xiansheng ji'nian ji* 巴金先生紀念集 [An essay collection in memory of Mr. Ba Jin], 442–43. Hong Kong: Hong Kong wenhui chubanshe, 2005.

Coetzee, J. M. *Stranger Shores: Essays 1986–1999*. London: Penguin Random House, 2001.

Dostoevsky, Fyodor. *The Brothers Karamazov*. Translated by Constance Garnett. Mineola, NY: Dover Publications, 2001.

Dostoevsky, Fyodor. *Crime and Punishment*. Translated by Constance Garnett. Mineola, NY: Dover Publications, 2001.

Eagleton, Terry. *Ideology of the Aesthetic*. New York: Blackwell, 1991.

Flaubert, Gustave. *Madame Bovary*. Translated by Eleanor Marx-Aveling. Seattle, WA: Amazon Classics, 2021.

Frank, Joseph. *Dostoevsky: The Miraculous Years, 1865–71*. Princeton, NJ: Princeton University Press, 1997.

Gao Xingjian 高行健. "Mei you zhuyi" 沒有主義 [Without isms]. In *Meiyou zhuyi* 沒有主義 (Without isms), 3–14. Taipei: Lianjing, 2001.

García Márquez, Gabriel. *Collected Stories*. Translated by Gregory Rabassa and J. S. Bernstein. New York: Harper Collins, 1984.

García Márquez, Gabriel. *One Hundred Years of Solitude*. Translated by Gregory Rabassa. New York: Avon, 1970.

Jerofejev, Viktor. "Daowang Suwei'ai wenxue" 悼亡蘇維埃文學 [Mourning Soviet literature]. *Shijie wenxue* 世界文學 [World literature] 2010 (4): 64.

Kafka, Franz. *The Castle*. Translated by Anthea Bell. Oxford: Oxford University Press, 2009.

Kafka, Franz. *Dearest Father*. Translated by Ernst Kaiser and Eithne Wilkins. New York: Schocken, 1954.

Kafka, Franz. *Franz Kafka: The Complete Stories*. Translated by Will and Edwin Muir. New York: Schocken, 1971.

Li Tuo 李陀 and Yan Lianke 閻連科. "Shouhuo: Chaoxianshi xiezuo de zhong-yao changshi"《受活》:超現實寫作的重要嘗試 [*Lenin's Kisses*: An important attempt at sur-real writing]. *Nanfang wentan* 南方文壇 [Southern cultural forum] 2004 (2): 20–29.

Liu Zaifu 劉再復 and Liu Jianmei 劉劍梅. *Gongwu Honglou* 共悟後樓 [Collaboratively understanding Red Chamber]. Beijing: Sanlian shudian, 2009.

Lu Hsun [Lu Xun]. *Old Stories Retold*. Translated by Yang Hsien-yi and Gladys Yang. Beijing: Foreign Languages Press, 1972.

Lu Hsun [Lu Xun]. *The True Story of Ah Q*. Translated by Yang Hsien-yi and Gladys Yang. Beijing: Foreign Languages Press, 1972.

Mendoza, Plinio Apuleyo. *The Fragrance of Guava: Conversations with Gabriel García Márquez*. London: Faber and Faber, 1988.

Rojas, Carlos. "Without [Femin]ism: Femininity as Axis of Alterity and Desire in Gao Xingjian's *One Man's Bible*." *Modern Chinese Literature and Culture* 14, no. 2 (Fall 2002): 163–206.

Rosa, João Guimarães. "The Third Bank of the River." In *Modern Brazilian Short Stories*, edited and translated by William Grossman, 125–30. Berkeley: University of California Press, 1967.

Salvidar, Dasso. *García Márquez: El Viaje a la Semilla* [García Márquez: Journey to the seed]. Salamanca: Universidad de Salamanca, 1997.

Shen Congwen 沈從文. *Biancheng* 邊城 [Border town]. Taiyuan: Beiyue wenyi chubanshe, 2002.

Tang Yongkuan 湯永寬. Postface to the Chinese edition of *The Castle*. Wuhan: Wuhan University Press, 1995.

Tolstoy, Leo. *Anna Karenina*. Translated by Rosemary Edmonds. New York: Penguin Classics, 1958.

Tolstoy, Leo. *Resurrection*. Translated by Louise Maude. Hertfordshire: Wordsworth Editions, 2014.

Wang Zengqi 汪曾琪. *Puqiao ji* 蒲桥集 [Pu Bridge collection]. Beijing: Zuojia chubanshe, 1991.

Woolf, Virginia. "Modern Fiction." In *The Essays of Virginia Woolf, Volume 4: 1925 to 1928*, edited by Andrew McNeille, 160–61. London: Hogarth, 1984.

Woolf, Virginia. *Mrs. Dalloway*. London: Vintage Classics, 2000.

Yan Lianke 閻連科. "Xunqiu chaoyuezhuyi de xianshi" 尋求超越主義的現實 [Seeking a reality beyond 'isms']. In *Shouhuo* 受活 [*Lenin's Kisses*], 207–9. Liaoning: Chunfeng wenyi chubanshe, 2003.

Yan Lianke 閻連科. "Xiezuo de pantu" 寫作的叛徒 [A traitor to writing]. In *Sishu* 四書 *The Four Books*, 229. Hong Kong: Mingbao chubanshe, 2010.

Yue Lin 岳麟. Preface to the Chinese edition of *Crime and Punishment*. Shanghai: Shanghai wenyi chubanshe, 1982.

Zhou Zuoren 周作人. "Ren de wenxue" 人的文學 [A humane literature]. *Xin qingnian* 新青年 5, no. 6 (1918): 575–84.

Index